To Romero -
Dragon Guide !
Kevin Gerard

DIEGO'S DRAGON

BOOK ONE: SPIRITS OF THE SUN

KEVIN GERARD

Crying Cougar Press™

San Diego, California

Published by Crying Cougar Press
San Diego, California

© 2010 Kevin Gerard. All rights reserved.
First published in 2011.

Edited by Katie Chatfield & the Penny Dreadfuls
Translations by Jose Jimenez
Cover art by Jennifer Fong
Interior illustration by Jennifer Fong
Typesetting by Julie Melton The Right Type

ALSO BY KEVIN GERARD:

Conor and the Crossworlds, Book One:
Breaking the Barrier

Conor and the Crossworlds, Book Two:
Peril in the Corridors

Conor and the Crossworlds, Book Three:
Surviving an Altered World

Conor and the Crossworlds, Book Four:
Charge of the Champions

Conor and the Crossworlds, Book Five:
The Author of All Worlds

Visit the author's website at:
www.diegosdragon.com

TO THE BEST STUDENTS ANYWHERE
CAL STATE SAN MARCOS
SOC36Ø RULES!

FOREWORD

Over the last four years I've traveled the country promoting another fantasy adventure series. Among the many readers I met, I saw thousands of Latino elementary and middle school students who were eager to read wonderful stories.

I began asking teachers and librarians about the availability of books with Latino boy heroes. I was shocked to discover that very few existed. Books with Latina heroes weren't plentiful, but they were accessible.

Many years ago I visited Rincon Middle School in Escondido, California. The librarian asked me to bring something special to give to a lucky student. After a lengthy contest, I gave Jorge Ramirez a handsome dragon statue I'd purchased at the Del Mar Fair. I congratulated him, we shook hands, smiled at each other, and that was that.

A few months later I entertained a couple of thoughts. The first was about this book, about how cool it would be to win a dragon statue at school and have it come to life. The other had to do with all of the wonderful Latino students I'd met over the years. I wanted to give something to them, a story with someone they could celebrate as their own hero.

This is the beginning of an amazing story for young readers everywhere. It is the first book in a new series called Diego's Dragon.

DIEGO'S DRAGON

BOOK ONE: SPIRITS OF THE SUN

CHAPTER ONE

Diego knew the dragon was alive the moment he touched it. Even though only a statue, and only eighteen inches tall, Diego felt a pulsing heartbeat when he accepted it from the author. The fiery blood racing through the sculpture almost burned his hand when he took hold of it.

Oddly, the man who gave it to him didn't seem affected by the life force surging through the statue. He was nice enough; after all, he had come to his school, stayed there all day and given him a cool dragon. Diego could tell the man loved the statue; he stroked the scales as he told the students so more than once during his talks. If he had felt what Diego had when he first touched it, he never would have parted with it.

The author shook Diego's hand, congratulating him in front of everyone in the library. Being a shy boy at heart, this startled Diego somewhat. However, he held his breath, looked the man straight in the eye, and thanked him with a smile. He reached forward, grabbing the statue at its base. A second later, he felt the energy rush forth from the dragon's legs. He looked at the author one last time and saw the man wink once before turning away. He walked to the desk to speak with the school librarian and the library tech. Diego found himself surrounded by a swarm of interested students.

"Diego, can I hold him?"

"Mijo, let me check it out."

"He's awesome! What will you name him?"

Diego set the handsome dragon down on a table in the center of the library. Two dozen hands reached out to touch the perfectly cut scales, the sharp teeth, the fanned wings. He allowed his classmates to touch his new prize, but he stayed close nonetheless. He felt a strange attraction to the dragon.

The eyes seemed to follow him wherever he went. Although none of the other students mentioned the dragon's gaze, Diego watched as the stunning, black eyes stared back at him with increasing interest. He moved in and out of the students swarming around the table, just to see if the tiny eyes would track him. As he stalked his prey, he watched to see if his dragon might wink at him.

He ran right into Racquel Carrillo, the prettiest girl in the whole school.

"I, I'm s-sorry," he said, stumbling over his words. Racquel's delicate brown eyes swallowed him whole. He lost the capacity to think. He looked at her, trying his best not to look foolish.

"That's okay, Diego," she said, looking at him playfully. Her smile nearly made him pass out. "He's a very fine dragon. Have you decided what his name will be?"

He recovered quickly, standing strong before her. "No, it will have to be a great name, so I want to wait a while and see what pops into my mind."

"How about Magnifico?"

He stared into her eyes, saying nothing.

"It's okay, Diego," she said, "just do me a favor and tell me his name when you figure it out."

"I will, I promise."

She waved and smiled. Diego felt his knees turn to jelly all over again. He wanted her to look back. He watched her so intently he barely heard Mrs. Coble calling to him.

"Diego!" she yelled for the fourth time. "Come over here with your dragon. We have to get some pictures. Aren't you excited? You'll be in the newspaper."

Diego reached through the crowd of students, wrapped his fingers around the dragon's body, and left a crowd of unhappy admirers in his wake. Some of them left the library; others followed him over to the desk.

"Now, we want to get a few pictures of you alone with the dragon," said Mrs. Coble, "and then of course some pictures of you with Mr. Sullivan."

The students began ribbing Diego about his sudden stardom. He took it well, but now that Racquel had left, he just wanted to go home. He couldn't get her out of his head.

"Smile, Diego," said Mrs. Coble, alarming him. "Hold your dragon up. Good, now once again, smile for the camera."

The picture session seemed to drag on for a month, first by himself, then with some friends, with Mrs. Coble, with Mr. Sullivan and Mrs. Coble, and finally a few with some other students. Diego began to get bored until he stood next to Mr. Sullivan for a set of pictures.

Unlike before, when he gave him the statue, this time Diego heard disturbing sounds that were either coming from his dragon or from Sullivan. He couldn't really tell which. He heard many dragons crying out close by, some happy, some terrified, some even wailing with anguish. The roars were light enough so that only Diego and Sullivan could hear them. When his picture session ended, Diego looked up at the man's face. He swore he saw flames flickering within his eyes. He stared, bewildered, as Sullivan smiled down at him.

At last, Mrs. Coble dismissed him.

Grabbing his backpack, he ran through the building and out into the quad. Moving from sunlight to darkness, and then to brightness again, Diego pushed through the gate that led to the street. He peered into the crowds of students waiting for their parents to pick them up. Then he looked through the windows of all the cars waiting in line.

He didn't see Racquel anywhere. He stood on the sidewalk with the dragon in one hand and his backpack in the other. He looked one last time and then backed up toward the gate. Leaning his body against the warm bars, he looked down at his new friend.

"If you can make her talk to me again, I'll keep you forever."

The dragon stared straight up into the sky, looking very much like a piece of molded plaster. The eyes no longer sought out Diego's gaze and the boy felt no heat coming from its body. Perhaps it *was* just a statue. In the excitement of the moment, Diego must have fed upon his own dreams and desires.

He saw his father's truck turn into the school driveway. Diego waved him over, walking toward the old Ford F-150 pickup. Unzipping his backpack as he went, he carefully stuffed the statue in the large compartment next to his books. He started closing the flap when he felt the zipper pulling against his hand. His backpack shook, quivering as if a cat was inside trying to escape. He tried slinging it over his back, but he couldn't maneuver it against the strange vibrations. As he neared his father's truck, he unzipped the main compartment again. The shaking stopped and the dragon sat inside the pocket, completely still.

"¿Mijo, qué pasa?" asked his father.

Diego lifted the statue out of his backpack and slung the loose bag over his shoulder. He opened the squeaky door of his father's truck and carefully climbed inside.

"What do you have there, Mijo?" asked his father.

"I won it at school today, Papa. It's a statue of a dragon. Doesn't he look fierce?"

"Si, muy furioso," he replied. "He is a very handsome fellow, as well, muy guapo."

"All of the students wanted it. A writer came to school today and gave out the prize for the best essay for the whole school district! I won. Can you believe it?"

As Diego's father pulled onto the surface street, he ruffled his son's hair. He felt so proud of him. "Really? That's terrific, mijo! You never cease to amaze your mother and me. First, you win the school math competition, then you make the honor roll, you bring home wonderful grades every year, and now this? Do you think maybe we should have a party, eh, a fiesta to celebrate little Diego's good fortune?"

"Papa, I'm not little anymore. I'm in the sixth grade. How many times do I have to tell you?"

"Sorry, mijo," said his father. "You're my youngest child, my little niño. I don't ever want you to grow up."

"How come, Papa?"

"Because, you're my little Diego, don't you see? You're my son, but you'll always be my little Diego!" He rubbed his hair again.

Diego smiled. The old Ford rumbled down the road toward his neighborhood. He looked over at the man driving the truck. He felt lucky. He loved his Dad a lot.

CHAPTER TWO

The day had started innocently enough. An announcement signaled Diego's winning entry from the month long, school-sponsored writing contest.

"May I have your attention, please? The winner of the author's dragon statue is Diego Ramirez!"

He'd written a gripping paper about World Cup soccer tournaments and how the competition instilled pride in the populations of countries around the world. At the end of his essay, he shared a personal story about his family's love of the Mexican national team, and of how he hoped to meet the players some day. Diego's principal sent his story to the local paper with a personal request for an article to appear the day they announced the winner.

The buzz about which student would write the best essay had been building for weeks. Each time a new class entered the library, the students walked by the dark, smoky statuette. Whispered compliments shot forth as each student glanced at the prize.

"Cool!"

"Awesome claws!"

"I hope I win it!"

The dragon stood about fourteen inches tall. The scales coiled closely around the body of the beast. The wings, flared out to their fullest extension, created a sense that the dragon would take flight at any moment. The column of spikes on the back of its head revealed a line of imposing weapons. The dragon's gaping mouth, filled with giant, tapering teeth, seemed to be calling out to an unknown master. He struck a handsome pose, gripping his pedestal with powerful claws.

Diego recalled how the author, Nathan Sullivan, told the story of how he brought the statue to the district offices as an enticement for students to enter the contest. He explained that it had sat on his desk the entire time he wrote his latest fantasy series. He'd considered it somewhat of a muse, for every time he got stuck he would always look into the dragon's frozen gaze and receive inspiration.

He told the children that the library services director had given him the idea to bring the statue along when he visited the schools. Diego remembered Mr. Sullivan talking about reading her email and the moment he'd caught sight of the fine-looking dragon. Sitting quietly on his desk, the black beast seemed to tremble with excitement at the prospect of traveling to meet the students.

He told them he'd left it up to his dragon. "You really want to go?" he had asked. "After all these years, do you really want to leave me?"

He said the dragon stared at him with an unwavering eye. The wings, although frozen on its body, appeared ready to come alive if he commanded. As he stared at his old friend, Sullivan had sensed something amazing. It looked alive, almost vibrating with anticipation. It seemed as though it was ready to fly to the schools on its own if he decided not to take it along with him.

"All right," he had said, showing the students how he'd stroked the scaly nose. "I'll miss you, but we'll see if some young writer can find inspiration with you on his or her desk."

He said at that moment the vibration ceased. The dragon's wings settled. It stared at him, and the author told them he'd seen a playful grin appear on its rigid face.

CHAPTER THREE

That evening, a celebration occurred at Diego's home. Happy voices from his family and friends filled the front yard. The men tended the beef and chicken roasting on spits. The kitchen smelled of fresh tortillas, salsas, tamales, and a huge salad topped with green onions and cilantro. Atop the kitchen counter, sodas for the children accompanied tequila and cerveza for the adults. Lively music poured out into the yard through the screens in the living room.

"Diego, let's go see it," said his friends, Jose and Ricardo. "You promised to show it to us!"

"I also promised my father I'd wait until after dinner. You can see it then, with everyone else."

"No," said Ricardo. "We want to see it now."

Diego did not want to displease his father, but he was dying to show the dragon to his best friends. It had stayed in his room all afternoon and into the evening without a visitor. He couldn't keep it a secret any longer.

"Okay, okay," he said. "I'll show it to you. But you have to swear you won't say anything to anyone until I bring it out after dinner."

"Okay," both the boys said together.

"Swear," said Diego.

Both boys swore on their souls they would not utter a word. Jose crossed his fingers behind his back.

"Okay, then, c'mon."

They passed through the kitchen on their way to Diego's bedroom. Each boy suffered through an endless barrage of female hands slapping his shoulders and running delicate fingers through his thick, dark hair.

"Oh, Diego," said one of his aunts. "I feel sorry for all the girls at your school."

As the ladies giggled, Diego ducked under her hand. His aunt turned to the rest of the ladies. "Have you ever seen a young boy so handsome for his age?"

A chorus of agreement followed Diego, Jose, and Ricardo. "Si, muy guapo, and his little friends, too."

The three of them ran down the hallway, eager to get away from the women and their silly compliments.

Diego shut the door to his bedroom. Holding a finger to his lips, he turned, silently telling his friends to keep quiet. When he saw their heads nod in agreement, he reached into his closet. He pulled an old pillowcase from the darkness. Jose and Ricardo could see that the cloth covered something big. They stayed where they were, sitting on Diego's bed, waiting to see the magical dragon everyone had described.

Both boys caught their breath after Diego pulled the pillowcase away.

"Awesome," whispered Ricardo.

"Magnifico," said Jose.

Diego jumped when he heard the word pop out of Jose's mouth. Was it a coincidence that Racquel had said the same thing this morning? He thought about the name for a moment and then discarded it. As he had explained to Racquel, he would wait a while to see what popped into his head.

"He looks so strong," said Ricardo. "Look at the wings; he looks ready to fly right now."

"Check out his face," followed Jose. "Look at all the spikes and scales. He's incredible, Diego."

Diego had to admit he had grown fond of the dragon as the day wore on. He must have checked the closet at least six times that afternoon, making sure it was still there. As he watched his two friends touching his trophy with wide eyes, he knew Mr. Sullivan had given him something special. *Maybe that's why he winked at me before he left the library.*

"Okay, he has to go back in the closet now."

Both boys responded together. "No, not yet."

Hard knuckles rapped against the door.

The three of them froze, staring wide-eyed at each other. Jose and Ricardo didn't breathe as they wondered who stood on the other side of the door. Diego's finger shot up to his lips again. He knew his father's knock when he heard it.

"Diegito?" asked his father, Alvaro. "Are you in there, mijo? The women are setting the table for you. Since you're the guest of honor, no one can eat until you've taken the first plate."

The door opened a crack. Diego stuffed the dragon in the closet and jumped forward to take the doorknob in his hand. He pulled it wide, smiling at his father.

"Papa, you could have just yelled from the kitchen. We would have heard you."

Diego's father looked at Jose and Ricardo. "Si, you are right, but then how could I catch you and your two amigos in the act, eh?"

"We weren't doing anything. Promise," said Jose.

Diego's father exploded in laughter. "Don't you think I was

eleven years old once? That's all you do when you're eleven – get into trouble!" His laughter began anew. He wrapped his arm around Diego's neck, holding him tightly in a headlock. He knuckled Diego's nose with his other hand as he dragged him down the hallway to the kitchen. He heard Jose and Ricardo running after them, laughing at his father's antics.

"Look who I found hiding in his room with his two friends," he said loudly.

The rest of the parents laughed with his father as the young man tried to squirm out of his grasp.

"Oh, no, little one, not until you are ready to take some food. I'm so hungry I could put my son's little friends on the spit right now." He let Jose and Ricardo rush by him. The two boys screamed with delight, laughing as they ran away from the man they all referred to as "Tio."

After his father released him, Diego grabbed a plate and ran to the front of the food line. He inhaled the variety of delicious scents rising from the table.

"Easy, mijo," said his mother, Alejandra. "You don't have to take everything at once. Seconds are allowed."

Diego smiled widely. He would do anything for his mother, but this was not a chore at all. He passed by the taco salad, heading straight for his aunt's tamales. He found the two largest and scooped them onto his plate. His eyes searched for his mother's chicken burritos next. He could eat them any time of day. He pulled four from the serving platter, spilling some of the sauce along the way. Next, he spooned some of his mother's Spanish rice onto his plate. He had little room left after the tamales and burritos, so he salted his entire plate with the rice. Lastly, he sprinkled tomatillo sauce all over the food.

"¿Qué pasa, Diego?" yelled one of his uncles. "Leave some food for the rest of us. We came to eat too!"

Another round of laughter poured through the windows of the kitchen.

A red-faced Diego ran from the table, followed closely by Jose and Ricardo.

"Get some food," cried Diego when they sat on a corner of the patio. "They'll let you go ahead of them."

"Give us a snack first," they both said, reaching for the small burritos on his plate. Diego stabbed at his friends' hands with his fork. It did no good, though, and soon all three boys ate the food together.

The evening progressed, with everyone enjoying the company, the music, and the endless trays of food. After everyone had eaten their fill and the plates had been taken away and washed, Diego's father and uncles brought out sangria and limoncello. Alvaro called for his son to bring out his prize.

"Mijo, tell everyone what happened at school today."

Diego stood, looking back down at Ricardo. When his friend mimicked wiping his cheek, Diego did the same, plucking a grain of rice from the corner of his mouth.

"A man who writes books came to our school today," he began. "He's been to every school in our district. He gave six talks in the library, and each time he reminded all of us about the writing contest sponsored by the schools. I've read some of his books. His name is Nathan Sullivan. He writes cool stories about dragons that come to life and hang out with kids like me."

He looked down at his friends for support. Jose pinched his ankle, urging him along.

"I was just waiting to leave school when they called my name.

I couldn't believe it at first. Out of all the papers written, mine was the best, so I won a dragon statue!"

Applause and cheers followed Diego's exclamation. Soon, cries to see the dragon rang out from the crowd.

"Run, Diegito," said one of his uncles. "Bring the dragon, rapido!"

"Come, Diego," said Alejandra. "Your aunts have been waiting all day. It's the least you can do after the fine meal they prepared for you."

When he hurried back to his bedroom, his family and friends slapped his arms and shoulders as he passed by them. Jose and Ricardo stayed behind, taking another trip through the buffet line. The adults stared toward the house, waiting for Diego to return.

Diego ran down the hallway. He threw open the door, letting it bang against the wall. A pile of clothing scattered on the floor slowed the impact a bit, but the noise was still loud enough to generate a few chuckles from the gathering.

Reaching into his closet, Diego felt around the area where he'd hidden the statue. Sensing nothing at all, he wondered if it had fallen to the floor. He had hastily stowed it away when his father knocked on his bedroom door. Falling to his knees, he reached back as far as he could, fishing through the clothes, toys, and school supplies.

He panicked. He couldn't find it anywhere. He wrenched the closet doors open, throwing everything that didn't feel like his dragon out onto the floor. He crawled into the dark space, hoping to find the statue tipped over against the wall.

How could he have lost it?

Jose! Ricardo! They were playing a trick on him. That had to be it! He would punch them silly until they told him where they'd hidden his dragon. He backed out of the closet, pushing everything back in as neatly as he could.

"Diego!" his father shouted. "What takes you so long, mijo?"

He turned toward the door, ready to run down the hall and confront his two best friends. He started forward but stopped suddenly. He stared but couldn't believe it. His dragon statue sat proudly on his desk, positioned so it could watch over Diego as he worked. It sat there, mute, strong, protective. A chill ran down Diego's spine.

His friends could never have placed the statue there without him knowing. He had looked back as his father carried him out of his room, watching them squeeze through the door behind him. The only way they could have tricked him was by coming back into his room before dinner, but they had been with him the entire time.

"Diego," called his father, walking down the hall toward his son's bedroom. "Where are you, mijo? Your friends and family are worried that you don't want to share your prize with them."

Diego stared at the dragon, shivering. Beyond the statue, carefully folded in thirds, lay the pillowcase he had used to cloak it. No one trying to play a trick on him would have had the time to place the pillowcase on his desk like that.

The young man's eyes flicked back to the statue. The dragon's eyes, shining with an eerie light, looked intently at Diego. The heat he felt the first time he touched the statue had returned as well. He felt it on his cheeks as he stared at the strange creature.

Diego nearly passed out with fright. His father looked in on him, laughing suddenly.

"Mijo, you look whiter than the sheets on your bed. What happened in here?"

"I-I just wanted to look at it a little longer by myself," he stuttered, "before bringing it out for everyone to see."

"Have you had enough time?" his father asked, still chuckling.

Diego took a step toward his dragon. The heat almost burned his hand as he reached out to grab it. He almost pulled away, but he didn't want to look weak in front of his father. Closing his eyes softly, he extended his arm toward the base of the statue. Prepared to have his hand horribly burned, he closed it around the hard plaster.

He nearly dropped it out of surprise. Nothing happened. The material felt somewhat warm, the same temperature as his room. He clutched the dragon to his chest and smiled.

"There, now," said his father, "that wasn't so hard, was it?"

"No, Papa."

"Good. Let's rejoin the family, then. I'm surprised they're not crowding the hallway wondering what happened to their little star."

It felt good to have his father with him. Diego had no idea what was happening; he was either going loco or something very special had occurred. He couldn't tell which.

As he burst into the kitchen carrying his prize, choruses of appreciation and admiration surged through the house. Diego set the statue on the butcher block in the middle of the kitchen underneath the blazing fluorescent lights. The dragon gleamed, its beautiful black coloring shining from every scale, horn, fang and claw.

"¡Extraordinario!"

"¡Precioso!"

"¡Muy guapo!"

"¡Magnifico!"

Diego snapped his head around upon hearing the last word of praise. Three times in one day was more than a coincidence. He looked in the direction of the remark but couldn't pinpoint the person who might have said it. The name, if it *was* to be the dragon's name, seemed to fall from the sky at the strangest moments.

"What will you name it, Diego?" asked his uncle. "It must be a strong name, befitting his character and demeanor."

"Yes, Diego," said another guest. "Tell us his name, so we might know how to address him when we visit your family."

"I'm not sure," said Diego. "I've only had him for a few hours. I want to give it some time so I can pick the right name." He looked at the glossy, snarling face of the dragon. *I should call you Timador because you are such a trickster.*

His father grabbed the statue from the butcher block. After giving it a good examination, he passed it to his brother. Many people took the opportunity to handle the precious dragon. They held it up to the light, caressed its wings, head and body, and a few even spoke to it. Diego watched with tempered anticipation until his statue came back to his father. His uncle, the last in the gathering to inspect Diego's prize, couldn't reach all the way to his father, so he leaned sideways to tap him on the shoulder with it. Just as he assumed an unbalanced posture, another of Diego's relatives threw his hands out wildly as he told a story to his cousin. Diego's dragon flew from his uncle's hand.

Diego watched with horror as his prize flew through the air toward the patio. His father hadn't noticed. He was engaged in a conversation with a different guest.

"Papa!" he called out.

"Hermano!" shouted his uncle.

His father turned just in time to lash out with his left hand. He gave it his best shot, trying to catch it, but the beautiful dragon bounced off his fingers and crashed onto the bricks of the patio.

"No!" screamed Diego.

The gathering, now tuned in to the crisis, gasped when they saw the statue smash against the hard brick. His father shouted to everyone to stand back. He tried to beat his son to what he felt sure would be many broken pieces, so he might gather them up and mend them before Diego saw his shattered statue.

The dragon bounced and rolled awkwardly, but did not break. Oddly, even though Diego hadn't been in its path, the statue rolled up to his feet at the end of its tumble.

Diego reached down to snatch the dragon from the brick patio. His hand stopped an inch away from the glistening, black body. The warmth had returned, but this time the statue seemed so hot he felt it might melt away to nothing. As he did before, Diego shied away from the intense heat. He hesitated only a moment, though, before lifting his dragon back into his arms. All he felt was the cool, smooth surface of the glaze. He smiled the smile of a boy both confused and fascinated by the events unfolding before him.

"How can this be?" asked his father. He reached down to inspect the statue, but Diego pulled it away. His father inspected it from afar, declaring the dragon unharmed.

"¡Magnifico!" declared his uncle.

"¡Excellente!" roared the crowd.

Everyone gathered at the home wanted to see the magic statue. They reached toward it, hoping to touch it while it lay within the boy's arms. Diego had other plans, though, and he raced into the house. With his two friends close behind him, he ran down the hall toward his bedroom. After the three of them squeezed through the doorway, Ricardo slammed the door shut behind them.

"Did you see that?"

"What just happened?" asked Jose.

"Let me see it," said Ricardo, "I want to smash it in the bathtub and see if I can break it."

"No!" shouted Diego, clutching the precious dragon to his chest. He let the statue fall away from his body so he could look into its piercing eyes.

The beast certainly looks fierce, he thought. *Is it just a statue, or is it something else? And what's the story with the strange man who came to my school today?* Diego shook himself from his thoughts, remembering his two friends. He didn't want to seem rude.

Just then the front door of the Ramirez home banged open. The windows rattled as the door slammed against the frame. A loud, drunken voice echoed down the hall. Diego looked at his friends with fear in his eyes.

"It's Esteban," he said. "He's come back again."

Chapter Four

Esteban hadn't always been so scary. Diego recalled many times when the two of them had spent days together just walking, throwing rocks and sticks, and greeting the neighborhood dogs.

Diego loved his brother, but he didn't like him much lately. For most of his life, Esteban wore a smile on his face. He had a great, booming laugh that Diego loved. It seemed every day he had a new joke for his little brother, and they never stopped playing and wrestling when they were home. Those were happier times.

Esteban changed after his girlfriend died in a horrible accident only a few blocks from their home. She had come to meet his parents and have dinner with the family. A delightful girl with magical brown eyes, Marisol impressed Alejandra and captivated Alvaro. The elder Ramirez gushed while saying good night to his son's girlfriend. His wife finally had to drag him away from the doorstep. She smiled and wished Marisol a safe trip home.

To Esteban, it seemed only seconds had passed when he heard the terrible sound of screeching tires, splintering glass, and the sickening crunch of twisting metal. Running like a wild man, he knew instinctively it was Marisol. He made it to the accident before any emergency vehicles arrived. He saw her small car bent backward and crushed underneath the heavy chassis of a tow truck. With one look, he knew his love had died.

Esteban seemed to give up on everything after that night. He stopped attending mass on Sundays, denying his mother's sincere and heartfelt urging. "It wasn't God's fault that Marisol was needed elsewhere," she had said. Nevertheless, he turned away from his savior, blaming Jesus for Marisol's death. He even accused his father of holding her at the house too long. Had he not been so talkative, perhaps Marisol would have left five minutes earlier and avoided the accident.

Worst of all, Esteban turned away from himself. He silently assumed all blame for her death. The erosion of his soul crept slowly along, destroying his mind and spirit. Diego had watched his brother change from a wonderful young man into some kind of tortured demon. He avoided him whenever he could.

Diego cringed as he heard his father confronting his brother. He held his statue tightly, certain that he would have to fight his older sibling for it.

"Esteban!" shouted Alvaro. "Why are you here? You no longer live in this house!"

Diego's brother swayed back and forth as he stared down his father. He reeked of beer and his eyes were ablaze.

"You have disgraced this family for the last time!" shouted Alvaro. "Get out before I throw you out myself!"

"Me?" slurred Esteban. "I'm a disgrace? That's so stupid it's not even funny. Look at you! You're just a fat, broken down, ex-foreman who can't even look at himself in the mirror."

The hand shot out quickly, slapping his son's face. The arm swung again, but Esteban, even though drunk, still had speed and strength well beyond his father's. He caught the hand roughly the second time, squeezing it until his father winced in pain. Esteban smiled wickedly.

"Esteban!" commanded Alejandra. "Release him at once!" She

clapped her hands together to emphasize her command. Her son obeyed, gazing at his mother with misty eyes.

"What do you want here?" she asked. "Why have you come home, now, of all times?"

"To see the great Diego Ramirez," said Esteban, "and his amazing dragon. Hell, the whole world's talking about it. One of my friend's little sisters told me this afternoon."

"You leave your brother alone," threatened Alvaro. "He doesn't want to see you and neither do we!"

Esteban started down the hallway toward the bedrooms.

"I'm calling the police right now!" shouted his father.

"Go ahead, maricón. I'll be long gone by the time they get here."

A group of Alvaro's brothers and friends appeared behind him by the front door. They offered their assistance should he wish to throw Esteban out.

"No," he said. "Let him go. Esteban may be in a bad way, but he loves Diego. He would never hurt him. It's me he can't stand."

Diego heard his brother's heavy footsteps coming toward his room. With only seconds to act, he frantically tried to find a hiding place for his dragon. He ran out of time when he saw the doorknob turning, so he quickly replaced the statue on his desk.

"Well," said Esteban, stumbling into the room, "if it isn't the three amigos." He held a fist out to Diego's friends, who returned the gesture lightly. Ricardo and Jose didn't like Esteban at all.

Esteban's eyes burned like a madman searching for prey. He looked left, then straight ahead, and then to the right. He saw what he had come for and reached forward as he took one lunging step toward Diego's desk.

"No," said Jose. "Magnifico belongs to Diego. You..."

Esteban swept his strong left arm toward Diego's friends. Jose caught the worst of it and fell back toward the closet.

Esteban turned toward the statue. The gleaming, black eyes of the dragon stared back at him.

"Magnifico?" he asked. "I like the name. I always wanted a dragon named Magnifico."

Ricardo started forward, but Esteban flashed his eyes toward him. The unspoken order stopped his movement.

"You don't mind, do you, little brother?"

"Would it matter, estupido?"

Esteban roared with laughter. He lurched forward with his right hand, clumsily grabbing the statue around the head. With a smirk fueled by a drunken stupor, he yanked the statue toward him.

The dragon didn't move.

Esteban nearly toppled over. He saw Diego and his two friends trying to cover their shocked smiles.

He took a stronger stance, balanced himself and pulled as hard as he could. His hand slipped, ripping away from the statue. He fell backwards against the closet door, cracking his head loudly.

"What the?" he asked no one.

With his feet in the air and his back against the carpet, he saw Diego, Jose, and Ricardo bent over in fits of laughter. He stared at them for a moment, finally exploding with laughter as well.

Diego's father kicked in the bedroom door. It slammed against the wall. He had been ready to unleash a tirade against his eldest son, but when he saw the four of them laughing like burros locos, he didn't know what to think. Seeing Esteban with a smile on his face took him back a few steps.

"What in the name of?" he stammered. "¿Qué pasa, Mijo?"

The four boys erupted into a fresh round of laughter. After a while, Esteban stood and pointed to the statue.

"I think Diego really wants to keep that dragon," he said. "He already glued it to his desk."

"Diego?" his father asked. He stepped past Esteban, reaching out for the statue. He grasped it easily, plucking it from the desk like a toothpick.

"¿Qué?" whispered Esteban.

"You're drunk," said his father, "and stoned, too."

The joy that had previously filled the room blew through the doorway like an angry ghost. Esteban's eyes narrowed. The laughter wrinkles disappeared. He stood slowly, staring at his father with daggers in his eyes.

His hand shot forward. He grabbed the statue, yanking it away before anyone could react. He made one move toward the door, when suddenly the statue jerked backward toward Diego's desk. It slammed down onto the hardwood top, and again, Esteban could not move it an inch. He tried and tried, but the dragon stared coldly while holding its place.

"Leave it alone!" shouted Diego. "It doesn't want to go with you! Get out of here and leave us alone!"

Jose and Ricardo smiled. Esteban shot a look at both of them. Then he pushed his father out of his way.

"Stupid statue," he said. "Who'd want a dumb thing like that anyway?"

"¡Vamos!" said Alvaro.

The four of them stood in Diego's room, listening to the front door open and then slam shut. Diego's father visibly relaxed when he heard Esteban walking up the driveway, singing to himself. He turned back to Diego and his friends, and the strange dragon standing in the middle of his son's desk.

"¿Qué pasa, Diegito? What's the story with your dragon? First out on the patio, and now with Esteban, are you doing magic tricks on everyone?"

"No se, Papa," said Diego, glancing at his friends and then back at his dragon. "It sat on the table all day in the library. Nothing happened at all, I swear."

"Nada?" asked his father.

"Nada," said Diego. "It's just a statue, that's all."

"Diego?" asked his father, sternly.

"Okay, Papa, something happened at school. When they announced my name as the winner of the statue, I came to the library to meet the writer. He shook my hand and handed me the dragon."

"And?"

"It felt as though the skin on my hand would burn away if I touched it. I was afraid, but I took it from him anyway. When I grabbed it the heat disappeared. It didn't burn me at all."

"Maybe we're all imagining things," said his father. "But maybe not. I'd like to invite this man over for dinner. Ask the librarian at your school to get in touch with him."

Diego slowly nodded his head. He would do anything for his father, but if it meant losing his prize statue, well, he would leave his home before he let that happen.

CHAPTER FIVE

The Escondido boys' club team was enjoying their first undefeated soccer season in seven years. With two games left on their schedule, they were facing a strong squad from Fallbrook. The pace had been maddening, with both teams racing up and down the field, trying desperately to win. With only a few minutes left in their match, neither team had scored a goal. The Fallbrook coach called time out and gathered his team around him.

Diego ran to his side of the field, grabbed a jug of water and poured it over his head. Jose and Ricardo did the same. The three of them toweled off as their coach knelt in front of his players.

"We might have to settle for a tie, boys. That's better than a loss. Let's focus on defense and protect our goalie. He's done a terrific job, but those Fallbrook players are really firing the ball right now."

Jose and Ricardo hung their heads. The other players looked to the ground.

"No, coach," said Diego. "We can win."

"I know you want to, Diego, but you're all spent. I can see it in every one of you."

"We're just trying to fool them," said Jose.

"Yeah, we're doing a good job of it, too," said Ricardo," elbowing his friend.

"Coach," said Diego, "we can beat them."

"How, Diego?"

"I know their winger. We played together last year. Get me one-on-one with him and the Fallbrook coach will send other players to help. That will leave our striker free."

"I don't know, Diego," said the coach. "We can't risk having half our defense trapped on their end of the field. Do you really think you can draw them off?"

"I know I can. I've been watching him all day. He's going to go at me, I can tell. Plus, he's tired. He won't make the right decision."

"All right, Diego, it's a risky move, but I'll let you run the offense. It's our ball, who do you want to toss it in?"

"Ricardo," said Diego. "Let him lag behind the other players and then come around my right side. That'll make them think we're going for a side kick with a header."

"And your striker is going to dash straight down the center of the field?"

"Yeah. Jose is faster than any of their players. After the time out, call a completely different play. Maybe that will confuse them."

The plan worked perfectly. With only ten seconds left, Jose slammed a shot into the back of Fallbrook's net. The Escondido boys fell all over each other, screaming, rejoicing and punching each other's shoulders. Diego squirmed out from underneath the pile and ran across the field. He sought out his old teammate.

"Hey, Dion," he called, loud enough for the Fallbrook bench to hear him. He ran over, extending his hand. "You played good today, hombre. I didn't think we'd have a chance against you guys."

Dion wrapped his arm around Diego's shoulder. "I almost told the team to back off when I saw Ricardo and you coming down the field together. That was a great scheme, Diego. Way to win the game at the last second."

"Jose won the game, not me. He runs like un demonio."

The Fallbrook coach congratulated Diego. He hustled his players together for a final talk.

"Adios, Dion," said Diego. "Let's hang out at the mall this weekend."

CHAPTER SIX

"Mucho gusto," said Alejandra, upon greeting Mr. Sullivan.

"El gusto es *mío,* Señora," he answered. He turned to Diego's father, shaking hands warmly and thanking him for the invitation.

"We are pleased to have you here, Mr. Sullivan. Why don't the two of us go out back and have a beer? If we're quiet enough, perhaps my wife will bring some tequila."

"I would be honored, Señor."

The two men left the foyer of Diego's home. As they walked toward the living room, Sullivan glanced down the long hallway toward Diego's bedroom. When he saw the young boy peeking around the doorjamb, he winked at him.

When they reached the backyard patio, he accepted a cold beer from his host. He waited for the man to seat himself before doing the same. They sat quietly for a moment, drawing on their bottles. The icy liquid chilled Sullivan's throat. It felt good to be in the company of someone who appreciated the simplicity of a beer in the early evening.

"The dragon you gave to my son," began Alvaro, "where did you find it?"

"I believe I bought it almost ten years ago from a street vendor in Del Mar. Why do you ask? Has something happened to it?"

"No, nothing. But something should have happened."

"What do you mean?"

"Maybe I'm getting old, or working too hard, and if it was just me, I probably wouldn't mention it."

Sullivan held the man's gaze, calmly urging him to continue his story.

"The other night we had a fiesta for Diego. It was the same day he received the statue from you at his school. By the way, I want to thank you for giving it to him. I've never seen him happier."

Sullivan smiled and then took a long drink.

"Everyone attended, lots of family, good friends, even a handful of students from Diego's school."

The author nodded.

"I'm not quite sure how to ask this," said Alvaro, "but is there anything special about that little statue?"

Sullivan reared back, spitting forth a full-throated laugh that echoed around the neighborhood. He tried to compose himself, hoping not to offend Diego's father.

"Why don't you tell me what happened during your party?"

"Yes, thank you," said a suddenly nervous Alvaro. "As I said, I may be losing my mind, but my brother, Diego's uncle; he saw this closely, as did my wife and two of her sisters."

"And Diego?" asked Sullivan.

"Yes, Diego saw everything." A note of excitement colored Alvaro's voice. "It was incredible! We dropped the statue onto a brick patio. It bounced and rolled, we thought surely it would break into a million pieces."

The author's eyes squinted slightly. "But it didn't?"

"No, no," said Diego's father. "Just the opposite. When Diego picked it up it looked as perfect as when he brought it out for everyone to see. No chip, no scratch, nothing."

"Hmmm," murmured Sullivan quietly. "I wonder," he said,

changing the subject completely, "has Diego come up with a name for his new statue?"

"I'm not sure, but different people at school and here in my home called it Magnifico a few times."

Sullivan smiled.

Just then, Diego's mother appeared with a bottle of Trago Anejo tequila and three glasses. One of the glasses glistened with a clear, silvery liquid. A small dish of salt and a bowl of sliced limes accompanied the fine liquor. She smiled at the men, announcing that dinner would be only a few minutes longer.

Alvaro deftly poured two fingers of tequila into the glasses on the tray. He passed one to his guest, gave the icy vodka to his wife, and lifted the other high into the air.

"Salud!" he said cheerfully.

"To an excellent host," said Sullivan.

"To an exquisite cook," added Alvaro.

They drank, smiling as they set their glasses down on the tray. Diego's father immediately grabbed the bottle to pour another round, but Sullivan gently held up his hand.

"I'll gladly share another with you later," he said.

Alvaro smiled broadly. He picked up his beer and asked his guest to do likewise. In the kitchen they could hear his wife calling them to dinner.

CHAPTER SEVEN

Diego sat in his room, doodling instead of completing his homework assignment. His dragon sat in the same place it had landed after Esteban yanked it away from his father. Diego had tried to move it, but the statue had other intentions. After his father had lifted it lightly away from the desk to show Esteban it could be done, the statue had assumed its solitary stance. After trying to move it many times, Diego now wondered if he had offended it. Perhaps it would stay there forever, just a block of plaster cemented to his desk.

When his mother called him to the dinner table, he ran down the hall thinking of nothing but his precious dragon. He'd forgotten completely about their dinner guest. When he saw Mr. Sullivan seated next to his father at their table, he stopped, startled, wondering what he should say first.

"Hello, Diego," said Sullivan. "I'm pleased to be here with you and your family. I hear your little dragon has been playing games with everyone."

"Si, I mean, yes, sir," answered Diego.

"Come on, Mijo," said his father. "Take a seat. No one here is going to bite you."

"Yes, please," said Sullivan. "Sit across from me."

Diego scraped the chair across the floor and sat. The smell of fresh tortillas steaming in their flat, round basket caused him to forget about everything but food. His mother was an extraordinary cook, and when they had guests for a meal, she spared no effort in making her table look appealing.

After his father gave thanks for their bounty, Diego reached for the enchilada tray. Alejandra rapped his knuckles with her fork, scolding her son for taking food before allowing their guest to partake.

"Diego Ramirez," she said, "this is how we raised you, to be a hog at the trough?"

"No, Mama," he replied. He glanced across the table. "After you, sir,"

"How wonderful it is to be young and have such an appetite," said Sullivan. "I can understand your urgency, Diego, I hope one day you will be as fortunate as your father and marry someone as talented in the kitchen as your mother."

Sullivan served himself a moderate portion of everything she prepared. After setting his plate in front of him, he gave the utensils to Diego's father, so Alvaro could serve himself next.

After everyone had filled their plates, the four of them silently consumed the scrumptious meal. Every minute or so a hand would shoot out toward the salsa or the tortilla bin. Other than that, no one said a word for quite some time.

Satisfied at last, Sullivan leaned back in his chair. "An excellent meal, Señora, thank you very much." He turned toward Alvaro. "And thank you, Señor, for inviting me to enjoy all of your home's delights."

Alvaro smiled broadly. Sullivan seemed at one with the world, a man used to many different people, and most likely many different places. He was very modest even though his writing must have given him reason to act otherwise.

"Diego, why don't you bring your dragon into the kitchen?"

Upon hearing this request, Alejandra rose from the table. She quietly removed the remains of the dinner, carrying the leftovers to the butcher block and the dirty dishes to the sink. While she cleaned, Diego ran down the hallway to his room, wondering if he would be able to lift the statue this time. As he somehow expected, it came away from his desk easily. He wondered if Mr. Sullivan had anything to do with that, but he shoved the thought from his mind and ran back to the kitchen. He excused himself as he moved around his mother, and set the handsome beast at the center of the gathering.

The table had been cleared and dressed for after dinner discussion. The tray with the salt and limes had returned, along with the attractive bottle of tequila. Alvaro had just poured another shot for Sullivan and himself, and a portion of vodka for Alejandra.

"Well, now," said Sullivan, reaching out to touch the dragon's neck. "What have you been up to around here, Magnifico?" As he glided his fingers along the finely sculpted scales, he could feel the dragon's tiny belly rumbling with appreciation.

"Seems harmless enough to me."

"Why did you call him Magnifico?" asked Diego.

"Is he not a magnificent creature?"

"Sí," said Diego, "he is muy guapo."

"Your father said that he and a few others called him by that name the other evening, when you first brought him home. It seems a fitting name for a dragon with his pedigree."

"What do you mean?" asked Alejandra.

Sullivan held his glass up, again saluting their warm home and the fine meal. After the three of them sipped quietly, Sullivan selected a lime slice, and after sucking the juice, he answered.

"In my profession I travel a great deal. I always try to take time to visit farmer's markets, bazaars, street fairs, anyplace where I might find something unusual. You see, I have many statues on my desk; dragons, gargoyles, candle holders, trees, more items than you can imagine. They help me with my writing, and, I might add, other aspects of my life.

"This dragon sat on my desk the entire time I wrote one of my adventure series. He was always there, urging me on, keeping me on track, or just laughing at me when I became too ridiculous for my own good.

"The street vendor who sold it to me was a most peculiar man. He seemed almost like a vagrant, penniless even. His stall looked very sparse."

"But this dragon was there?" asked Alvaro.

"Yes, in the middle of several piles of old clothing, costume jewelry, and a pair of black cats that seemed to be watching over it.

"I almost didn't ask about it, it seemed to be the most valuable possession the man owned."

"I'm glad you did," said Alejandra. "We can tell our son is quite taken with it."

"After watching me for a minute or so, the merchant waved the cats away from the statue. He picked it up and handed it to me."

The author threw back the last of his tequila. He licked his lips as he set the glass down on the table.

"I stood quietly while he talked at length about the dragon. He told me this little statue had taken quite a journey to find me. At first I thought he was pulling my leg, but as he continued describing all the places the statue had visited, I grew more trusting."

"Is this the truth?" asked Alvaro.

"Hush, mi amor," said Alejandra. "Let the man tell his story."

Smiling, Sullivan waited for their chat to end before continuing. He liked the Ramirez family; it was no wonder Diego was such a well-mannered young man.

"Apparently, Magnifico came into this world as one of many such statues produced in the Orient, Malaysia, I believe. After being polished and packaged, he fell into a distribution line. As his brothers and sisters shot off in various directions, to be shipped all over the world, this statue somehow escaped."

Diego looked at his mother, and then over at his father. All three smiled at the twist in the story.

Sullivan reached out to touch Magnifico. "I guess this dragon decided it was too important for his future to be left to chance. A worker in the plant found him only minutes before closing. She brought the statue to her superior, who was too tired to deal with one little piece. He told her to throw it away on her way out.

"Of course the woman kept it as a prize for her son. They lived in a fishing village near Kuantan, on the central coast of Malaysia. The child, barely six years old, rejoiced upon seeing the dragon. He'd never been given anything so grand in his life. He slept with the statue for days, keeping it tucked into his warm bed linens."

Diego smiled, thinking of the way he had held his dragon close the first night he took it home. As Sullivan continued speaking, however, his smile turned to a grimace of horror.

"Regrettably, the story of Magnifico's first home ends in tragedy. A month after the child received the statue, a powerful tsunami swept through the village, killing everyone. Everything the villagers owned either disappeared or was destroyed."

"A terrible story," said Alejandra.

"Yes, a tremendous loss of life." Alvaro crossed himself, with his son quickly following the gesture.

"Even with the destructive force of the tsunami, this little statue survived without a scratch. A relief worker found it buried under tons of trees and stones. They kept it at their headquarters as a talisman of good luck.

"The statue either became lost or found its way onto a freighter docked near the Strait of Malacca. After a lengthy journey, it finally ended up in Southern California, where I happened to be strolling along a boulevard one day. I felt very fortunate to have found him. He's brought me an untold amount of luck and prosperity."

"For you, yes," said Alejandra. "But for others, only tragedy and death."

"If you believe in that sort of supernatural tale," said Sullivan, smiling.

"Still, I'm not sure this statue is the right thing for our son," she said.

"Mama, no!" shouted Diego, a little too forcefully.

Sullivan noted the boy's passion, the way he pulled the dragon close to him, protecting it. *Good,* he thought.

"It is only a hunk of plaster, esposa," said Alvaro. "What harm can it do?"

His mother still had her doubts, but she deferred to her husband. Later that evening, however, in the privacy of their bedroom, they would have a serious talk about their guest and his peculiar gift.

"Why don't we ask Diego what he thinks?" asked Sullivan.

Diego watched as three pairs of eyes turned toward him. At first intimidated, he suddenly blurted out his response.

"Magnifico is mine! He was given to me! I won't give him away, ever!"

"With your parents' permission, of course," added Sullivan.

"Y-yes," he said, "with your permission, Papa, and Mama." His embarrassment could have lit up the night sky.

"Of course, Diego," said Alvaro. "We can all see how much you idolize your new friend."

"Well," said Sullivan, standing quietly. "I'm afraid I've overstayed my welcome."

"Not at all," answered Alvaro. "We've enjoyed having you in our home."

"Yes," said Alejandra, "aside from the amazing tale you shared with us, you've given Diego a wonderful gift."

"Hopefully it will inspire him to do great things."

"I'd be happy if it helped him clean up his room."

Laughing, everyone rose from the table. Diego's father led the author to the front door, his wife and son trailing behind.

"You are a generous host, Señor," said Sullivan. He grasped the man's hand warmly. "And I've never had finer Mexican food in my life, Señora." He shook her hand briefly before turning to Diego. "Take care of Magnifico, Diego. He will look after you as long as you never abuse him, or let anyone else mistreat him." Sullivan smiled and stepped through the doorway. "Buenos Noches," he said.

Diego and his parents said their goodnights before closing the door.

"Okay, Mijo," said his father. "Off to your room, you've already stayed up longer than you should. Take your dragon and get ready for bed."

"Then I can keep him?"

Alvaro looked to his wife for support.

"Of course you can keep him," she said. "Just remember what the author said. You must always watch over him."

CHAPTER EIGHT

Sometime during the night Diego woke, his pajamas damp with sweat. His bed sat in the center of a roaring fire. He watched the violent rush of flames as they swept up the walls of his bedroom.

His closet exploded in a flash. The fire swallowed every piece of clothing he had before flooding his bathroom with a vibrant, multicolored blaze.

Pictures flew across the room, disintegrating into ashes after bouncing off the opposite walls. Diego's desk rolled over onto the floor, destroying everything he'd worked on during the school year.

Magnifico, he thought. *Where was his dragon? Had the fire consumed him as well?* He peeked over his covers, which were becoming warm from the embers falling from the ceiling.

Just before swinging his legs onto the floor, he caught sight of Magnifico floating in the center of his bedroom. A shiver trickled down Diego's spine as he looked at the dragon's eyes. They were the color of the fire burning in his room, and Magnifico did not resemble the harmless statue Mr. Sullivan had given him. Diego swore he saw one of the wings unfold, stretch out, and then collapse again. Even with the heat from the embers, he cowered under his covers.

A wave of fire swarmed up from the floor onto his bed, consuming the blanket his grandmother had finished crocheting for him the day he was born. Diego pulled his feet up to his waist, keeping his toes from being burned along with his mattress.

Suddenly, the walls of his bedroom caved in. The heavy brick crumbled under the intensity of the fire, and Diego threw the remaining covers over his head, hoping by some miracle that the firestorm would somehow pass him by. When he felt the searing heat of the flames tickling his feet, he screamed as though his life depended on it.

The last thing he saw in the bizarre dream world was the image of Magnifico spreading his strong wings over his bed, protecting him from the horrible flames. He did the only thing he could imagine; he curled his body underneath the dragon's protective umbrella. When he felt the fire burning his body from all sides, he screamed for his father to save him from the inferno.

His bedroom door creaked open.

"Mijo?" said his father. "Everything okay in here?"

Diego threw his bed covers forward. He flung his hands toward the foot of his bed, slapping the bed linens covering his feet. He saw the fingers of the fire licking his legs and arms. He flailed against the flames, panicked, trying to save himself from being burned alive.

"Mijo?" his father asked, clearly concerned now. He saw nothing but a child wrestling with a nightmare. He entered the room, hoping to wake his son before anything else scared him.

Diego cracked his eyes open and looked at his father. He threw his arms around the sturdy shoulders, hugging him fiercely. He wanted to cry, but the memory of the horrible flames kept flickering in his mind. He just held on, feeling the soothing safety of his strong arms.

Suddenly, his father's body warmed to a very uncomfortable

temperature. It became increasingly hotter, until finally Diego pushed himself roughly away from him. When he looked at his father's face, he screamed again as the nightmare continued. That face, always so calm and serene, had turned into a mask of terror. Eyes blazing and mouth distorted, it wanted only one thing, to scare Diego senseless.

Then it changed. The skull melted and then reshaped itself into Esteban's face. Instead of a mask of fright, the new face showed intense pain, even fear. It called out to Diego, asking him for help, begging him to save him. Seconds later, the head dissolved like sand running through an hourglass. The body disappeared in a similar manner, pouring over Diego's bed and onto the floor.

In its place the roaring fire resumed. Shooting straight through the mattress and covers, it rose from the floor like a funeral pyre. Diego scrambled back toward his pillows, but there would be no escape this time. The fire engulfed his bed. He felt his pajamas starting to burn. He cried out for his parents to help him. In a last gasp of anxious hope, he looked over at his desk. Magnifico was gone, most likely burned alive by the flames. Diego closed his eyes, waiting for the blaze to devour him.

A shadow rose up beyond the foot of his bed. Broad and imposing, it blocked the light from the flames. Diego wanted to peek through his tightly shut eyelids, but he felt too afraid. His cheeks burned with the heat of the flames. The deafening roar of the fire rattled his nerves. His throat rasped as he coughed harshly. He began to despair, thinking his situation was hopeless.

A voice called out to him. He knew the owner of the message, he felt certain of that. Mr. Sullivan, maybe somewhere within the blazing walls of his bedroom, was asking him to look straight in front of him.

He couldn't understand why, but he followed the man's instructions. First, he cracked them only a little, which yielded nothing but blackness. Then Diego opened his eyes wide. He gasped at the sight, beautiful and terrifying at the same time.

Magnifico stood at the foot of his charred bed. Perched on the frame by his immense, talon laden feet, he nearly brushed his spiked head against the ceiling. He spread his wings out to either side, fanning the flames creeping up toward Diego. Finally, with a horrifying roar, he brought the wings forward, slamming them together.

Anything previously untouched vanished within the thrust of the dragon's mighty wings. The blast wave slammed against Diego's small body, knocking him against the headboard. Diego's reflexes forced him to lower his chin and shut his eyes for a brief second. When he opened them again, the wall of fire rushed toward him.

A second later, he looked out across a vast desert. He saw nothing for miles in every direction but the whirls of sand and dust rising on the horizons. He thought it might be only wind, but he felt no draft. He did hear the unmistakable sound of horses, hundreds of them, pounding across the desert toward him.

Minutes later a column of riders reached him. He stood his ground, watching the strange men racing by on their oddly packed horses. They looked like something out of the history books at school. Each man was heavily armed, riding with one hand grasping the reins and the other holding a rifle. Battle cries hit Diego's ears; they called out in Spanish, prodding each other along.

One rider separated from the pack. He veered toward Diego. Switching his reins to his rifle hand, he held the other low along his saddle. He swooped in, yelling at Diego to take his hand. Diego reached high, grasping the strong arm as the horse rumbled by.

A second later, he rode behind the man, holding his gun belt firmly.

A rousing call went up from the Mexican riders. Shots rang out. The rifles recoiled as scores of bullets flew forward.

A bullet zipped past Diego's head. He looked to the side, watching riders fall, horses tumble as the opponent returned fire.

The man guiding Diego's horse tossed his rifle to the ground and ripped two pistols from their holsters. As he began firing Diego saw the column of enemy riders flash into the scene. Madness followed. Men and horses fell in groups all around Diego. Bullets flew in every direction. Screams of victory and agony rose with the dust flying toward the sky.

The rider Diego clung to took two bullets, one in the shoulder, the other in his side. He faltered briefly as he tried to swing his horse away from the battle. He yelled loudly, commanding his troops to retreat. Suddenly, he slumped against Diego, letting the reins fall to the saddle.

Diego reacted without thinking. Reaching around the man's side, he gathered the reins in his hand. Lashing them against the horse's flank, he yelled as loudly as he could. The horse shot forward, carrying Diego and the wounded man away from the battle.

The other Mexican riders caught up to their leader. They cheered Diego's courage, firing shots into the air and yelling his name. Two galloped close on either side of Diego, making sure Zapata didn't fall from his saddle.

Diego looked behind him as the group ran to safety. When he turned forward again, he saw a wall of fire consuming the entire desert. The riders neither slowed nor tried to veer away. As the horses stormed toward the flames, Diego slammed his eyes shut.

When he opened them his bedroom stood as it was before.

Everything; his clothing, shoes, closet doors, curtains, everything sat quietly where it had been before the inferno had erupted. Nothing seemed out of place, and no scent of fire danced around Diego's nostrils. He couldn't smell a thing, and his bed seemed as fresh as the day his parents bought it for him.

Even though Diego expected the worst, he jerked his head to the left, flicking his eyes toward his desk. He exhaled for the first time since the bizarre dream began. Magnifico, his handsome dragon, sat quietly, the strong wings curled around its black, scaly body. Its mouth remained open, howling at some annoyance only it understood.

Diego jumped when he heard a light tapping at his bedroom door. It opened just a crack, revealing his father's smiling face.

"Mijo, I wanted to check on you before going to bed. Can you sleep okay? Can I get you a drink of milk?"

Diego stared at his father with wide eyes. Just as in the dream, he waited for his smiling face to change into a twisted, laughing demon.

"Mijo?" his father asked.

"No, Papa," he said. "I'm fine. I just needed to think for a while before going to sleep."

"Okay, Mijito, as long as you're alright." Diego's father pushed open the door. He walked to his son's bedside, leaned down, and kissed Diego's forehead. "Hasta mañana."

"Night, Dad. Thanks for letting me keep Magnifico."

His father smiled. "So that's his name?"

"Yes," said Diego, smiling. "I like it. It is very powerful."

"Es muy macho," his father said, marching around in a circle. "Macho Magnifico," he said, pounding his chest and making funny faces. Diego laughed aloud at his father's antics.

"What's going on in here?" asked his mother, standing in the doorway. "Are you acting the fool again?"

Diego and his father exchanged a quick glance. His father skulked out of the room, mimicking a hen-pecked husband. His mother came to his bedside. She tucked him in as only a mother can do. Kissing his nose, she brought the comforter up to his chin.

"Sleep well, my little Diego. I'll make you a special breakfast in the morning."

"Waffles?"

"Si, with pecans and cinnamon."

Diego reached up and hugged his mother hard. He loved her more than anything in the world. She always knew exactly what to say, what to do, and how to tell what he needed in any situation.

He rolled over onto his side. He heard the bedroom door close very softly. His mother would never do otherwise. He carried the warmth of that thought along with him as he drifted off to sleep.

CHAPTER NINE

"Diego, Diego!" screamed Racquel as she ran across campus. She had forced her mother to drive her to school early so she could lie in wait for him. When she saw him, she rushed over to his father's truck.

"Diego!" she said, half out of breath. "Oh, hola Señor Ramirez."

"Buenos Diaz, Bonitita," said Diego's father. He nudged his son as he exited the truck. His devilish smile made Diego blush with embarrassment. He jumped out of the truck, slammed the door, and walked toward school with Racquel.

"Diego!" she said, excitedly. "I had the most incredible dream last night!"

Diego knew exactly what she would say next.

"Your dragon!" she continued. "He was in my room! Last night! He saved me!"

Diego's knees turned to jelly.

"There was a fire in my room, everywhere, I couldn't escape it!"

He looked at Racquel as if she were a stranger. Alarm bells rang in his mind. He suddenly felt dizzy.

"You should have seen him," she said, "he was huge, like a giant eagle, except all black, the way he looks now!"

"Ohhhh," he groaned.

"Diego?" asked Racquel. "Diego, what's wrong?"

By this time they had passed through the gates that surrounded the school. Diego led both of them to a bench by the library. He practically fell down on the seat. Racquel grabbed his arms, steadying him. She looked into his eyes with great concern. They seemed dead almost, distant, unfocused.

"Diego, talk to me!"

"I, I had the *same dream* last night."

"What?"

"Mostly the same, anyway," he said. "My room almost burned to the ground. My father came in to help me, except he turned into my brother and then dissolved like sand pouring through your fingers. The flames almost had me. They were starting to burn my pajamas. I closed my eyes, but I heard Mr. Sullivan telling me to open them. When I did, I saw Magnifico at the foot of my bed. Huge, just like you saw. He clapped his wings together and sent me to some desert, where I saw a bunch of soldiers fighting a battle. I even joined in for a bit. It was strange but it also seemed so real. As soon as the battle started, it ended, and I landed back in my room.

Racquel stared at her friend, dumbstruck. She didn't know what to say.

"This whole thing is becoming a little scary," said Diego. "I'm thinking about getting rid of Magnifico."

His statement snapped Racquel back to life. "No!" she screamed, a little too loudly for where they were sitting. The students walking in the halls looked over at them. "You can't do that."

"It's just a statue."

"You don't really believe that, do you? After what happened last night?"

Diego looked around the school. He spoke quietly to Racquel. "Other things have happened, really strange things."

"Don't you see?" she asked. "You've been given some kind of gift, something very powerful."

The first bell rang, telling students it was time to go to their homerooms. Diego had five minutes left to talk with Racquel. He didn't want her to think badly of him, but he had to tell someone.

"I'm afraid of Magnifico," he said, "afraid of what he might do."

"What do you think he'll do?" asked Racquel.

"I don't know what he'll do," said Diego, "that's what scares me."

"I'm sorry, Diego, really sorry about everything. Everyone felt so happy for you when you won the statue." She stood, picking up her backpack in one motion. "I have to go to class. You do, too."

"Listen, Racquel," he said quickly, "I want you to help me get rid of him. Meet me after school today, right here, and we'll talk about it."

She smiled, running down the hall. "Okay, Diego, after school."

As Racquel approached her classroom, she grasped the pendant her mother had given her on her last birthday. She fell against the wall in the hallway, uttering a short prayer only she could hear. She kissed the blessed mother on the face of the pendant and closed her eyes.

"Don't worry, Catalina," she whispered. "Soon you'll again be among the living. If everything works out, my brave Diego and his dragon will open a doorway between worlds. You will walk through and live among your family again. I promise."

At two fifty-nine, Diego gathered his belongings into his backpack. If Mrs. Seawood had seen his eagerness to leave, she no doubt would have made him stay behind for violating her classroom rules. He couldn't help himself, though. Two things danced around in his mind, Magnifico and Racquel. He couldn't forget his fear about the strange statue, or the way he felt about Racquel. At least Magnifico had gotten her to notice him, he could be thankful for that.

When the bell rang, Diego flew out the door. He heard Mrs. Seawood screaming for him not to run. He ignored her as he dipped and dodged through the students walking in the hallway. He wanted to find the bench before Racquel did. He wanted to be waiting for her when she arrived.

When he rounded the corner by the front gate, he saw Racquel with her little group of friends. His heart skipped a beat as he wondered whether she had told them about her dream. *It could be all over the school right now if she even told one person,* he thought.

She turned and smiled, saying hello to Diego as he walked up to her. Her friends all smiled, greeting him warmly. Soon afterward Racquel said her goodbyes. She grabbed Diego's sleeve and dragged him around the corner by the bathrooms.

"This is the coolest thing ever," she said. "Magnifico, I mean, and by the way, I'm glad you gave him that name. It's very strong."

"You didn't tell anyone, did you?"

"Of course not, silly. Did you?"

"No," said Diego. "I don't want anyone to know. I'm going to get rid of him today, and you're going to help me."

"How are we going to do that?"

"Tell your mother we need to study together for an exam, or that we're working as a group on a school project. Get her to drive you over to my house after school. Tell her my parents will be home and one of them will drive you back to your house later this afternoon. Tell her you'll be home for dinner, that way she'll say yes."

"Aren't you the devious one," said Racquel.

"Just do it! I need your help with this."

"Okay, fire-breather, just calm down. I'll help you. You're almost like that dragon yourself."

"Sorry," said Diego, "I'm just nervous about getting rid of Magnifico. What if he gets mad and wants to take it out on me, get revenge or something?"

"Diego, it's just a statue."

"Yeah and we both had the exact same dream last night. Just a coincidence, right?"

"Here comes my Mom, and I see your Dad's truck only a few cars behind her. You want me to come straight over, right?"

"Yes, we have to do this while it's still light."

"Where are we taking him?" asked Racquel.

"To the dump," answered Diego, "where else?"

They had walked almost five miles from Diego's home. He told his parents they were meeting other students at the library. When his father insisted he drive them, Diego fumbled with an explanation about a fitness program at school. He wanted to walk, as did Racquel. After a long, suspicious look, his father agreed to their departure.

"Okay, Mijo," his father had said. "Just be careful."

They had crossed the invisible line separating the suburbs

from the city a mile back. The smells, stress levels, air quality, even the clothing people wore were vastly different here. Diego knew exactly where the garbage trucks went at the end of their runs. His father had been a supervisor there before starting his own contracting company. For some reason, as a small boy Diego loved riding around in his father's work car, especially when it came time to return to the site.

Diego led Racquel around one last corner. The tall, rusted fence line of the dump loomed across the street like a medieval fortress. Diego and Racquel recoiled as the smells of the site assaulted their noses. The noise of the trucks and tractors working inside the fence muted everything else around them. Diego shook his head, wondering how he ever could have loved such a stench.

He walked Racquel right to the entrance. There, a man sat in a small booth controlling a gate that allowed trucks to enter and leave the grounds. Every driver had a special sticker on his or her windshield. When the guard saw that the identification looked current, he would open the gate and let them pass.

This was exactly what Diego had planned for when he decided that the statue would go to the dump. He hadn't hoped to enter the grounds. He knew the guard would never let Racquel and him cross that line, no matter what position his father used to hold.

Racquel took one whiff of the garbage going by in front of her and gagged. She slapped a hand over her nose and mouth. When Diego looked over, he saw that she had become quite pale.

"Don't worry," he said, "we'll be gone in a minute."

When the next truck pulled in and stopped at the gate, Diego removed the statue from his backpack. After the gate creaked up to its standing position, the truck's brakes hissed as the driver released the pedal. The filthy truck heaved forward, noisily bouncing over the tracking for the gate.

Diego waited until the back of the truck presented itself. He flicked his eyes at the guard to make sure he wasn't watching, and then tossed Magnifico into the grimy, smelly muck.

The truck's compactor pressed down on Diego's statue.

CHAPTER TEN

Nathan Sullivan was napping with his feet up on a cushioned ottoman when he felt a strange pull on the farthest reaches of his mind.

It had been a perfect afternoon. He had accomplished a great deal of writing earlier in the day, a new proof had arrived in the mail, and a UPS driver had dropped a shipment of Offley Port on his back patio. He opened a bottle immediately, pouring a generous serving for himself. After a leisurely glass of the delicious reserve wine, he fell into a comfortable afternoon of carefree sleep.

The message had come through, however, loud and clear. Something had gone terribly wrong. Nathan quickly stood, careful not to disturb anything on the teakwood deck outside of his bedroom. He walked through the French doors, silent as a shadow, carefully descending the stairs down two floors to his writing study. He checked his computers, wondering if he'd received any messages. He found none.

Ignoring the keyboard, he placed his right hand flush against the blank monitor. Instantly, the screen came alive, but what appeared there had never shown up on any other computer in Diego's world.

Bizarre names flashed across the screen. As each one appeared, an eerie trail of blood stained print followed along. At least twenty names flashed on the screen at any one time. He watched closely; he was looking for one very important student.

"Diego," he whispered. "What have you done?"

The clanging in his head increased. He hopped down another flight of stairs and walked briskly across the room. He waved his hand in front of a very simple looking door. As he did so, he uttered a short phrase. A lock clicked and the door opened. The author entered the small room, closing the door behind him. He leaned on the handle, making sure it was secure.

He turned, softly walking through the cushioned carpet of the soundproof room. At the far end sat a compact altar. The author knelt, heels under thighs, as he had been trained. He waved his left hand over the middle of the altar. This time he whispered a more complex spell, something no one but he would understand.

He rested both hands on his thighs, continuing the incantation. A moment later, the altar vanished, leaving him kneeling in front of a blank wall. He chanted, calling for some type of deity.

Suddenly, a thousand voices cried out from within the wall. A multitude of bizarre forms glimmered, dancing in front of him. Every few seconds a collective roar of dragons would expand in volume and strength.

Sullivan's incantation ceased. He sat silently. With his eyes closed, he waited for the wailing spirits to give him some type of signal. He did not have to wait long. Although the souls of the dragons remained, their shrieks died away.

"Rise," spoke a single voice. "Sit comfortably and tell me your story."

Sullivan did as the voice commanded. He took his time reseating himself. The dragons stirred, anxious to hear the tale.

"The guide has withdrawn," he said. He breathed the words softly, waiting for a violent reaction, but nothing within the wall challenged him.

"The *chosen* guide?" asked the keeper of the dragons' spirits.

"Yes, my master. I do not understand why."

"Perhaps you selected the wrong candidate," argued the keeper, suddenly irritated.

"No," said Sullivan. "Diego is the proper guide. Even if I hadn't thoroughly researched his background, I would've known the instant I saw him."

"What has he done?"

"He is afraid. The dream terrified him. It is my mistake. I showed him too much too soon."

"What has he done? *Don't force me to ask again.*"

"Magnifico is gone," said the author. "Diego has cast him into a horrible place."

The combined roar of the dragons shook Sullivan's home to its foundation. The wall before him began to crumble, torn apart by their agitation.

"I will not punish him this time," spoke the furious voice within the flurry of spirits, hearts, and souls. "See to it that he never forces my hand again."

"As you desire," said Sullivan. "What am I to do about Magnifico? I fear he is lost forever."

"Leave him to me," said the keeper, settling into a less threatening tone. "I will see to our dragon and his guide."

Sullivan bowed. "Most capable one, I will do everything you say. As always, I bow before your wisdom."

Sullivan assumed the obedient position once again. He closed his eyes, listening to the bellowing dragons as they faded into the magical vessel. When he felt certain his master had vanished completely, he allowed his thoughts to drift without direction. Listening to every sound, inhaling the scent of the dragons' altar, and touching the carpet beneath his hands, he pressed his forehead to the ground. In this position he was able to free his mind completely.

He recalled the first time he'd been confronted by a dragon. As a young, struggling writer, he often fought with distractions. Sometimes he sat staring at his monitor, trying to pry anything from his mind, any type of sentence at all. He would slam his fist on his desk, jarring everything. He'd throw his hands out in disgust, knocking over whatever happened to be within reach.

On one particular day, he toppled a dragon statue he'd bought the week before. It flew over the edge of his desk, clattering across the hardwood floor. He rose from his chair, only to sit, or rather fall back into his seat. With both fear and awe, he watched as a small dragon, identical to the one he'd just badly abused, rose up from the floor on tiny but sturdy wings. A startled chirp emerged from the dragon's mouth, warning Sullivan never to mistreat a member of the Sol Dragones again.

To his amazement, Sullivan understood the dragon's language. Overcoming his shock, he cupped his hands underneath it and helped it back to his desk. Once comfortably situated again, the dragon told Sullivan its story, a tale the author swore he'd never relay to another soul.

The Sol Dragones lived within the fiery soul of the sun, the birthplace of the inhabitants of every universe. From the beginning of time, they had been called upon to nurture, guide, and save the lives of peoples on an infinite number of worlds. After each journey, they returned to their birthplace to rejoice with each other. Their service brought untold happiness to people of every description, on planets near and far.

In the early years of the sun's formation, the master of the Sol

Dragones proclaimed that one attendant on each world would be summoned to work with a single dragon. This being would act as an agent, a seeker, the one appointed to locate the proper guide to assist the dragon with its duties.

Sullivan remembered the exact moment when he realized he had been appointed as agent for earth. After telling him its story the small dragon increased in size, almost breaking through the roof of his writing room. Without warning, it bathed him in magical fire. It sung the ancient songs, chanting in a way that mesmerized him.

After the ritual ended, the dragon assumed its original position on Sullivan's desk. Becoming rigid again, it spoke its last words.

"We will call upon you when necessary. If you serve with humility, your life will be enriched a thousand fold."

Sullivan allowed the phrase to repeat itself in his mind as he brought himself back to the present. Only then did he press against the plush carpet with the palms of his hands.

He pushed himself up into a sitting position, rolled his toes underneath his feet, and stood. He took his time, stretching each group of muscles as he awoke from his trance.

He walked up the stairs to the top floor of his home. Using chairs, bookcases, and doorjambs to brace himself, he made his way back out to the deck beyond his bedroom. He plopped his body onto the Adirondack chair. He looked at the beautiful glass of port. The clear cylinder gave way to the glossy purple liquid. With the sun dropping in the sky the color contrast became even more striking.

When he felt he could, Sullivan strained his stomach muscles and leaned forward. Holding his left hand out to block the piercing sunlight, he grabbed the glass and brought it to his lips. He inhaled the delicious aromas of the fine port before draining the glass in two lazy sips. Each time, he let the velvety liquid lie on his tongue for a few seconds, so his taste buds might enjoy each distinct flavor.

The communication, combined with the effects of the alcohol, caused the author to become quite sleepy. He lay back in the chair, closed his eyes, and allowed his mind to ponder the situation. Just before he fell into a deep, dreamless sleep, a single thought floated through his mind. *Oh Diego,* he thought, thinking about the last words of his master. *You have no idea what you've done.*

CHAPTER ELEVEN

Diego heard Mr. Recker calling on him. "We are trying to learn about the branches of government in the state of California." The rigid man stalked over to Diego's desk. "Can you tell us, please, how many seats there are in the state assembly?"

"Eighty?" asked Diego with a bored expression.

"Precisely," said his teacher. "And how many constituents does each member represent, on average?"

"Over four hundred thousand?"

"Very good, Mr. Ramirez."

Diego watched Mr. Recker walk briskly away from his desk. Undoubtedly, he'd seen his student daydreaming for the first half hour of class, and Diego knew he wanted to catch him without a reply. As had happened so many times before, the answers came easily to him.

As the class continued, Diego found himself staring out the window more and more. He had become more despondent ever since the day he and Racquel took the statue to the dump. Acting on impulse and fear, he had tossed away a magical gift as if it were a toy.

He missed Magnifico. It had been almost a week since their trip to his father's old workplace. If he could find a way – but it was ridiculous – even if he knew where to look, he would have to dig through mountains of rancid, stinking garbage. On top of that, the machinery at the dump had probably ground the dragon into dust

58

by now. There was no way around it. He had thrown away the best present he'd ever received.

When the bell for lunch rang, Diego mindlessly turned in his assignment and stumbled out the door. He looked up and down the hallway for his friends and for Racquel. The two of them hadn't spoken but once since their trip downtown. Diego found his thoughts drifting in her direction more than a few times. He missed seeing her, and he had only himself to blame. If he had kept Magnifico, perhaps she would have...

"Diego Ramirez," the loudspeaker blared above his head. "Please report to the library at once. Diego Ramirez, come to the library immediately."

Shaken from his thoughts, Diego started jogging in the direction of the library. He waved to a few friends as he passed the soccer fields. Perhaps he might have time for a game at lunch. Maybe that would get his spirits back up again.

As he raced around the corner by the library, he ran smack into Racquel. Her books flew in three different directions. Her papers exploded from her arms, circling out of their reach. Diego tried to mumble a broken apology, but Racquel stopped him cold.

"Diego!" she said, clearly shaken. "How did you get it back? You did go back for it, didn't you?"

If she didn't look so pretty, Diego would have brushed past her on his way to the library. He just couldn't look away from her glorious, brown eyes. He did, however, see quite a few students standing by the building's double doors.

Racquel socked his shoulder. "Well, did you?"

"What are you talking about, girl? Did I *what?*'

"Magnifico, silly, he's in the library, right now, sitting on Mrs. Coble's desk!"

Diego's heart started pounding. He had to fight to breathe normally.

"So, you didn't bring it back from the dump?" asked Racquel, watching Diego's face lose all its color.

The loudspeaker crackled again. "Diego Ramirez, come to the library immediately. Diego Ramirez, please come to the library."

He wanted to run off the school grounds and never look back. There was no longer any doubt. Mr. Sullivan had given him something spectacular, a dangerous and magical beast.

"Come on," said Racquel, "you better go see what she wants."

CHAPTER TWELVE

Diego couldn't feel his feet from that moment on. His mind spun out of control. Every thought slammed together against his skull like a pinball machine gone mad.

He heard none of the students' greetings as he entered the library. He felt none of the hands clapping his shoulders and back as he moved through the small crowd of students. He half saw the stacks of books as he moved deeper into the library. As he came around the anti-theft bars by the back door, he saw the librarian discussing his statue with a large group of students.

"Diego was nice enough to bring his statue back to school today. You can see he's taken excellent care of it. Look at how the black finish shines in the sunlight! And the scales and horns, look how magnificent they are! He truly is a very handsome dragon."

Diego walked around Mrs. Coble's desk, stopping in mid step. He shook his head, opening and closing his eyes. He stared at his statue, not believing what he saw. It seemed bigger, stronger even; his body shook as he walked around the group of students looking at his dragon.

Although it maintained its silent stillness, something tugged at Diego's mind. He could feel the life bristling inside the plaster coating. He thought it strange that none of the other students seemed to notice. They had all gathered around, talking in small groups and reaching out to touch Magnifico, but no one had remarked about his bigger size and stature.

"Diego?" asked Mrs. Coble. "Are you going to leave your prize here for a few days, or do you plan to take him home tonight?"

"I don't know, I..."

The words stalled in the back of his throat, almost gagging him. He looked in horror from Mrs. Coble to his dragon. The plaster that formed Magnifico's body shook and twisted. The horns bent, the teeth gnashed, and before Diego's eyes, Magnifico broke free from his shell.

The dark, scaly face turned in his direction. The eyes blinked, the head shook, and a high pitched, eerie wail poured out through the spiked teeth.

Magnifico bobbed up and down on his muscular legs. He flapped his leathery wings, stretching them until Diego could almost see through the skin. Craning his head left and right, he looked at the crowd of students standing around him.

He threw a warning snarl at two students standing a little too close. A tiny stream of bluish flame shot forward through his sharp, gnashing teeth. One of the students held her hand up, pointing it at the statue. She leaned in, intending to touch the dragon on the nose. Magnifico responded by rearing back into a striking position.

"No!" yelled Diego as he launched himself toward the student. He tackled her to the ground a split second before Magnifico lashed out with a vicious snap. Diego heard the resounding click of the powerful jaws as they clamped down on nothing but air.

"Diego Ramirez!" said Mrs. Coble sternly. "Have you lost your mind? Rosa merely wanted to touch the statue. You surprise me; I should think you'd want to share your wonderful prize."

Diego released the girl. She stood quickly, adjusting her clothing before moving far away from him. Diego stared at Magnifico, watching him playfully snap at other students in the library. He wanted to scream.

"Stop it!" he hissed. "Are you loco?"

No one in the room can see what I can, he thought. To the rest of them, Magnifico remained a statue, nothing more. He stood, shaking his head again.

"If that's the type of behavior we can expect from you, Mr. Ramirez, I suggest you take the dragon home with you this afternoon."

"Si, estupido," said Ricardo, poking Diego in the back with a pen. "I thought you liked Racquel, anyway."

"I do," he said, clearly unnerved. "I wanted to save that girl from..."

"From what?" asked Jose, "the magazine rack?"

The two boys' laughter made Diego's nerves unravel a bit. They had left their games and raced to the library after hearing the announcement for him to report. Arriving seconds before Diego's masterful performance with Rosa, they nearly lost it when she and their good friend hit the floor of the library.

"What's got you so spooked?" asked Ricardo.

"Don't you see?" asked Diego.

"See what?" asked both boys together.

"Look!" Diego pointed his finger at Magnifico.

"En qué, amigo?"

The ill-mannered dragon watched the exchange between his guide and the other two boys. As well as a mysterious monster could, he laughed at Diego's predicament. Then he hopped across the table toward Ricardo, clacking his talons against the wood surface.

"Don't you see that?" asked Diego.

"Shhh," said Mrs. Coble. "This is a library, not a playground!"

"Sorry," said Diego. He turned to his friends, whispering harshly. "Look, look at what Magnifico is doing *right now!*"

Jose and Ricardo turned around. They took one look at the dark, motionless statue and then turned back to Diego.

"You loco, muchacho," said Jose.

"You better pray for forgiveness," added Ricardo.

Before Diego could say another word, Magnifico moved to the edge of the table closest to Ricardo. Spreading his wings as wide as they would stretch, he filled his lungs with air. A second before he could belch out a fiery plume, Diego reacted.

"Magnifico, no!"

He tackled his friend to the ground. It was the second time in less than five minutes he had completely disrupted the peace and quiet of the library.

"Mr. *Ramirez!*" shrieked Mrs. Coble. "What on earth is going on?"

Ricardo pushed his friend to the side and stood. Both he and Jose hurled fresh insults at Diego. Then they stepped over him on their way to the library door.

Diego lay there, frozen, not believing anything that had happened since he entered the library. He even doubted his own sanity. He watched as dozens of students walked by him, looking down and snickering as they left the building. He turned and saw a twisting line of smoke curling up toward the ceiling.

Mrs. Coble came around her desk. She walked resolutely across the room until she stood directly over Diego's prone body. She grabbed the lifeless statue from the table top, shaking it at Diego as she spit out her orders.

"If I ever see this statue in this building again, I'll take it to the trash compactor in the faculty lounge and grind it into nothing." She set Magnifico back down on the table and crooked a finger at Diego. "You should be ashamed of yourself, Mr. Ramirez. You embarrassed us. You made a mockery of a great gift and of this library. Now, you take this statue and keep it with you for the rest of the day. Then, after school, you take it home and don't ever bring it back here again. Is that clear?"

Diego stared up at the librarian, stunned.

"I said, is that *clear?*"

"Si, I mean, yes, Mrs. Coble."

The librarian turned in a huff and walked back to her desk.

Diego lay on the floor, not quite sure what to do. From his vantage point, he looked straight up at the edge of the table. He closed his eyes and sighed when he saw a tiny spurt of flame shoot out over the top of the wooden surface. Then he heard the unmistakable sound of sharp claws scraping across the old, rough, wood. Two seconds later he saw Magnifico's scaly, spiked head peer over the top of the table. The dragon looked, cocked his head the other way, looked again, and then spoke to him for the first time.

"¿Qué pasa, Diego?"

CHAPTER THIRTEEN

For the rest of the day at school, four more periods to be exact, Diego kept Magnifico locked away in his backpack. He didn't dare reach in there for a pen, a book, or even a piece of paper for fear that el dragon loco would spring through the zipper and turn the classroom into a free for all. All he'd need after the episode in the library would be another embarrassing scene. He could just picture Magnifico flying all over the room setting fire to everything that would burn. He would chase him like a lunatic, pushing through desks and knocking everything over. Then the teacher would pick up a harmless statue and ask him what in the name of creation he was doing. Diego could barely pay attention to any of his lessons.

Magnifico didn't make it very easy for him. Diego felt certain he hated being cooped up in the dusty pocket with the horrible smells of pens, pencils, and lined paper. He heard him discover the remains of a delicious snack Diego's mother had given to him that morning. Magnifico made a tremendous effort to eat the tasty morsel as loudly as he could, causing half the room to stare at Diego as if he were the offending party.

Every time Diego tried to get comfortable in his chair, Magnifico shot out a leg or a wing, giving him a good whack on the back or in the ribs. Diego tried desperately to act normal whenever he received these little reminders. It was difficult due to the dragon's strength.

66

Whap! He would feel the horned tail slap against his spine. After his body reacted to the impact, Diego would keep turning in the same direction to cover his reaction, smiling at other students noticing his bizarre behavior.

Oomph! One of the dragon's powerful legs would shoot out, connecting with Diego's kidney. He would grimace, and then smile, acting the fool to the student directly to his right.

"Mr. Ramirez, are we feeling ill today?" asked one of his teachers. "You may be dismissed if you'd care to go see the nurse."

Diego thought about that potential scene. The nurse would no doubt ask him to remove his backpack and set it on the floor. Of course, Magnifico would free himself and blow fire onto everything in sight. The flammable liquids would explode, the nurse would freak out, the school would be emptied and the fire department would show up.

"No, Mr. Beadles," he said. "I'm fine here. I'm just sore from soccer practice, that's all."

"Fine. Please see to it that your outbursts do not disturb the other students."

After Diego's teacher finished his comment, Magnifico bit right through the heavy backpack and sunk his teeth into his guide's shoulder. It was everything Diego could do not to cry out. He sat there, sweating. A second later, his eyes glazed over.

He rubbed his eyes, bringing them back into focus. Instead of his classroom, he looked upon an old hacienda filled with people. Some were dressed like the fighters he saw in his dream. Others looked more business-like, with slacks, ironed shirts, and vests. Many men spoke at the same time, trying to yell over each other.

"War is the only thing they understand," claimed Zapata, a general in the Mexican army.

"It is true," said Villa, a revolutionary and freedom fighter. "Negotiation with the northerners will bring us nothing. It will only give them more time to arm themselves. We must attack now, while they are wounded."

"Gentleman," said a wavering vision of Benito Juarez, a scholar and leader in the early anti-colonial movement, "I would gladly fight alongside you once you are left with no other alternative, but you must give others time to speak to the northerners. You have fought courageously, but they are many more than we, and soon they will win this war by sheer numbers if nothing else."

"They're weak," said Zapata. "They know nothing of fighting on the plains. We should take every man we have and hit them tonight. If we attack while they're planning, it'll be better for us."

"I agree," said Villa. "I say we vote, now."

"I urge you to follow a different course," said Juarez, his ghostly body fading slightly.

"We vote," said Zapata and Villa.

The men in the room held their hands high when asked for their opinions. With one hundred twenty six present, sixty-three voted for war and the same number for negotiation. After a moment of frustration, the entire assembly turned their attention to Diego. Juarez pointed a glimmering finger and asked, "You, Diego Ramirez, if you intend to save our people, tell us what we should do, and tell us why you treated Magnifico so poorly!"

CHAPTER FOURTEEN

The final bell rang, signaling the end of school for the day. Diego ran down the hallway, hoping beyond hope his father would not be late picking him up. Even though the hallways swarmed with students, he saw no one as he raced past the classrooms toward the school's entrance.

Magnifico did not care for his shenanigans one bit. Bouncing around inside the backpack, he kicked, scratched, and bit anything that felt familiar to him. At one moment he found the exact place he had bitten Diego in the classroom. He opened his jaws wide and clamped down, finding the same holes he had previously made.

"Ouch!" yelled Diego. He flailed his hands around behind him, completely missing his target. Magnifico sunk his teeth in deeper, finding a bit of humor in his guide's behavior.

Finally, his father's truck turned into the driveway leading to the pick-up area. He waved at Diego. Waiting patiently for the other parents to gather up their children, he inched forward toward his son.

"Hola, Mijo," he said as Diego climbed into the truck.

"Hi, Papa." He pulled himself toward the middle of the cab, leaning forward and removing his backpack. He nearly punched Magnifico for all the trouble he gave him today. Instead, he rested his hand on what now was a very rigid statue. Diego, startled for a moment, kept his hand where it fell. He actually began to calm down, now that Magnifico had assumed his lifeless form again.

"I wanted to thank you for what you did for me today," said his father. "I thought that little dragon of yours would never leave your side again."

Diego's head slowly turned toward his father. With chills racing down his spine, he asked the question.

"What do you mean, Papa?"

"Magnifico," said his father. "You left him on my desk this morning with a note saying I could take him to work if I wished."

Diego's throat went dry. He touched the bulge in his backpack, fingering the texture of the wings. He swallowed as well as he could under the circumstances. He almost felt too afraid to find out what happened.

"You kept him at work all day?"

"Si, everyone came in to have a look. Magnifico held up marvelously. He showed his best side to each person who visited him."

Diego squirmed as small beads of sweat began dripping down his back. He didn't know whether he should ask his father or not. It wouldn't make sense after what he saw at school.

"What do you mean, he showed his best side?"

"To everyone who came in to say hello. No matter which side they looked at, or even if they walked around and around him, he always seemed to shine the brightest on whatever side they were on."

Diego exhaled, slumping down a little farther into the seat. At least he hadn't come alive in his father's office. If he had there would have been a three alarm fire in ten seconds.

Whump! Diego felt one of Magnifico's feet thump against his back. He leaned on the backpack, hoping to disguise any movement. The last thing he wanted was to have to explain Magnifico's pranks to his father.

He felt his cell phone buzzing in the front pocket of the backpack. He fished it out and popped open the cover. He had one text message – from Racquel. He almost deleted it; his worst fears raced around in his head like a hurricane.

"Aren't you going to look at it?" asked his father. "You kids always have those things open, it's loco."

Diego pressed the sequence of buttons. Racquel's message popped up in the inbox.

"Diego! Magnifico's here, in my room!"

"Who's it from?" asked his father. "What does it say?"

"Just Ricardo," he lied, his voice quivering. "He wants to know about tonight's homework."

Another message popped into the inbox. Diego brought it up. "Diego????"

With trembling hands, he tapped out a return message.

"Sorry, Racquel. Don't touch him, or do anything. I'll call when I get home."

Diego's father turned his work truck into the wraparound driveway at their home. He pulled as far out the other side as he could before stopping and grinding the gears into reverse.

"*Whew!* Permiso," he said, pretending the gear noise was him farting.

Diego laughed. It was the first time in hours he had felt good about anything.

"Thanks, Papa!" he said as he raced toward the house. He reached for the door handle, leaning his shoulder into the heavy wood. He almost fell flat on his face when his brother opened it first.

"Hah!" said Esteban, obviously drunk. "Look what I found." He held a black dragon statue in his hand. Gloating over his younger and much smaller brother, he held the statue aloft, just out of Diego's reach. Diego jumped up and down, trying to knock it out of his brother's grasp.

"Esteban!" roared his father. *"¿qué hace usted aquí?"*

The eldest son sneered at his father. "I came here because I was hungry, not that you would care."

"I told you never to come back here, never!"

"Well, I did. What are you going to do about it?"

Diego's father was a thick, heavyset man. Even in his early forties his arms and chest were well muscled. He had held back from physically confronting his son up to now, but to have Esteban challenging him, well, that just didn't go over very well.

He charged Esteban, pinning him against the rock wall the two of them had built during happier times. He rolled the palm of his hand across his son's chin and then braced his thick forearm against his throat. He leaned forward, locking eyes with the son he'd named after his own father.

"You're choking me," garbled Esteban.

"I'll do more than that if you ever show your face here again. Give Diego his dragon, now!"

The hand holding the statue came down as ordered. With tears in his eyes, Diego took it from his brother. Even with everything that had happened, he loved Esteban. It hurt him so much to see his brother and father locked in combat.

"¡Basta!" screamed Diego's mother. *"Stop it I said!"*

Both men sensed the terror in her voice. Diego's father released Esteban with one final shove against the jagged rock. He backed away, breathing heavily. Esteban straightened his clothing, pulling harshly on his shirt and jacket as he stared at his father.

"Esteban," said his mother forcefully. "Go to wherever it is you call home." She swallowed hard. "Your father is right. Don't ever darken our doorway again."

The look of pain on Esteban's face hurt Diego deeply. Fathers and sons nearly always battled during their lifetimes, but the loving bond between mothers and their sons held firm through anything. Esteban held his throat as he looked at his mother. The tears she shed made his flow more freely.

"How could you say that to me, Mama?"

"Go," she cried. "Please, just go."

With one last angry look at his father, Esteban turned, jammed his fists in his pockets and stormed down the driveway. His three family members watched him go.

"I'm sorry, corazón, I..."

"¡Idiota!" said Alejandra. "¡Estupido! You attack our son like an animal, have you lost your mind?"

"He deserved it for what he's done!" yelled Alvaro. "He disrespects you, he taunts his little brother, what do you want me to do, give him a pat on the back and a reward?"

Diego didn't hear his mother's scolding or his father's response. He even lost sight of his brother, who had just hopped the fence at the end of the driveway. The only thing he saw was his right hand, which a second ago held his dragon statue firmly. It was gone, and his clenched fist gripped nothing but air.

As his mother and father continued bickering, Diego reached down and grasped the zipper of his backpack. He could tell before he opened it what he would find, or wouldn't find, rather. He threw the flap back and stared at his books, pens, and calculator.

"¡Mierda!"

Diego's mother and father stopped their squabbling immediately. Neither one of them had ever heard their younger son swear before. They were so shocked they didn't have a chance to say anything before Diego raced down the hall to his bedroom. He slammed the door and opened his cell phone in one motion.

"Racquel, is he still there?"

"What, Diego?"

"Is he still there?"

"Magnifico?"

"No, Don Francisco! Yes, Magnifico, is he there?"

"Not any more," said Racquel. "As a matter of fact, he disappeared just a few seconds ago."

CHAPTER FIFTEEN

Esteban Ramirez slapped the eucalyptus leaves as he stormed down the trail by the river. He found a large, partially hidden branch in a pile of shredded bark.

Taking the slim end into his hand, he began swinging the club at the smaller branches hanging down from the eucalyptus trees. He liked shredding the leaves and chopping the branches in two. When he felt angry, as he did now, it made him feel good to take it out on someone else, or something else. In a fit of rage, he smashed the sturdy branch against a large tree trunk, shattering it into dozens of pieces.

Even in his furious mood, the destruction of the trees haunted him. When Diego and he were small boys, they walked this trail together many times, climbing the huge trees, waiting for unsuspecting hikers to approach. Taking the tiny seedlings from the leaves, they would drop them from their lofty chairs and try to bounce them off someone's head. They were so high in the trees that even if their targets became angry, they usually couldn't find them, and if they did spot them, they'd never be able to climb up and get revenge.

Sometimes they'd just sit and let the wind rock their perch back and forth. They would talk for hours about anything - school, friends, family, anything at all.

Esteban never let on about how proud he was of Diego, whom

he considered the smart one in the family. He loved his little brother and always protected him from bigger boys.

He picked up some chunks of concrete, one at a time with both hands, and flung them over the fence. He watched them roll and hop down the hill, finally splashing into the shallow, slow moving stream at the bottom of the man-made river. After a few tosses with no spectacular results, Esteban continued his walk among the trees.

Damn su padre, he thought, kicking a small rock up the path. *It wasn't like he didn't take a drink or two every night.* He ran his fingers through his hair. He felt painfully conflicted. He both loved and hated his father. He hated his stubbornness, his rules, and his inability to feel empathy for anyone else's situation. The man had an iron will, and once he made up his mind about anything that was it.

Esteban still blamed his father for Marisol's death. The asno mudo wouldn't let her leave the night she came to his parent's house for dinner. Marisol was lovely, and his father, like most men, could not resist the smile of a pretty, young girl.

He had swallowed more than his share of tequila that night. When the evening ended, he kept hugging Marisol, telling Esteban how lucky he was to have found such a joya. His mother tried to pull him away many times. Esteban, seeing the discomfort on Marisol's face, had finally ripped his father's strong arm from his girlfriend's shoulder.

Esteban swore, kicking wildly at another rock. Missing it cleanly, he almost lost his balance. As the rage burned hotter, he threw his arms about, slashing at anything within reach. As many times and as hard as he tried to push the anger out of his mind, he knew he would never be able to. He simply couldn't dismiss the blame he felt for his father. *It was his fault,* he thought, striking out at a branch. His fingers came away bloodied from the small but tough knots on the eucalyptus leaves.

After his father had finally released Marisol, Esteban insisted on driving her home. He would walk back to his parents' house, he said. Marisol refused, kissing him lightly on the nose. She turned her hypnotic eyes up toward him, told him she loved him, and got into her car.

Esteban had bent down, sticking his head in the window for one more kiss. She complied, and then pushed his head away. She told him to give his father a kiss goodnight for her and drove off. It was the last time Esteban saw her alive.

Damn him! He wiped his bloody hand against his pant leg and then swiped at another thick stream of leaves.

As much as he hated his father for what happened, something else tore at Esteban's heart. He tried hard to deny it. He drank heavily every day since the accident, hoping to mask the pain of a memory that burned his soul to ashes. Each time the thought flicked into his head, he shoved it aside. Sometimes the shame was so great he would throw out his arms and scream, hoping to scare the truth from his mind.

In the early morning hours, after a long fit of drinking, his mind would go numb. The painful thoughts would recede like the tide of a lazy ocean. It was here, in the stupor of alcoholic bliss, that he found a little peace before passing out.

Esteban could not forgive *himself* for that night. He placed the blame at his father's feet more for self preservation than anything else. Yes, the man kept Marisol longer than he should have, but Esteban felt no less guilty. After his mother had wrestled his father into the house, Esteban had delayed Marisol's departure by a few precious moments. If he hated his father, he hated himself a thousand times more. He had killed Marisol as much as his father had. If he hadn't delayed her departure that night, who knows what might have happened.

He woke screaming her name every morning. The pain of losing her fought with the throbbing hangovers for control of his mind.

Esteban reached into his pocket. He fumbled around with a handful of change before pulling out a few bills. *Seven dollars and eighty seven cents,* he thought, *enough for tonight, anyway.*

He turned toward the city after leaving the tree-lined trail. He would do as he always did, follow the riverbed until it ran into another waterway. He would walk along the new bike path until the sun sank low on the horizon. After the night cloaked the sky he would find the nearest liquor store. Perhaps he'd be able to steal a package of beef jerky to eat with his beer.

He zipped up his jacket, pulled the collar up around his neck, and put his night face on. It was a good idea to look tough after the sun went down. Anyone who saw him would think twice about trying to rob him.

He looked up at the sky, eyes wide open. *"Marisol, mi corazón, where are you?"*

CHAPTER SIXTEEN

Diego sat on his bed, eyes and mouth wide open. They had gotten rid of the statue, and yet it had reappeared everywhere. First in the library, then with his father, and at Racquel's house, he didn't know what to think. He'd carried it home from school in his backpack, but now, along with all the others, it too had vanished.

He grabbed his cell phone and called Racquel.

"Where was he?" he asked her.

"The statue was on my desk. It just appeared out of nowhere. I saw it when I came home from school. I called you right away."

Racquel sounded more than a little frightened. It had all been a game until today.

"No one could move it, not even an inch," she continued. "I hit it with my softball bat *as hard as I could.* It didn't move at all, and it didn't even get scratched. I dented my bat but nothing happened to Magnifico."

"Racquel," said Diego, as calmly as he could. "It's okay. Everything's going to be okay. He's gone now, anyway, right? All of the statues have disappeared."

"What do you mean all of them?"

Diego cursed himself for his stupidity. He'd almost calmed her down and now he'd blown it.

"Racquel, the statues were everywhere, even at school. Maybe Magnifico's trying to tell us something."

"Or maybe he's really ticked off and he's just playing with us right now. Who knows what he'll do next."

She's right about that, thought Diego. After what he saw today at school, he didn't know what to expect.

"Look," he said, "Let's not worry about it. If he is going to do anything, I'm sure he'll come after me. After all, I was the one who threw him in that stinking garbage."

"Diego, I'm afraid."

"Don't be. Let me call you in the morning, right when I get up. That way, we'll both know we're okay."

"Okay, Diego. Don't forget."

"I won't."

"I'll talk to you in the morning," she said.

"Racquel?"

"Yes?"

"I'm glad for one thing at least."

"What's that?"

"I'm glad Magnifico brought us together."

"Me too, Diego. Goodnight."

"Buenos Noches, Racquel."

Diego slapped his phone shut and tossed it onto his bed. He reared back when he saw it bounce wildly off the blanket and slam against the ceiling. Suddenly unable to breathe, he glanced over at his bedroom door as it quietly closed itself. His bathroom door did the same.

He almost lost it when the sliding glass door leading out to the pool slowly glided shut. The locking mechanism turned clockwise by itself. Then the room sat silently.

Diego mastered his fear, replacing it with anger. He was tired of all the games. If the dragon wanted to kill him, then so be it. He dragged his desk chair out so he could sit down. After a few minutes of silence he spoke.

"Come out and show yourself, dragon! I'm tired, hungry, and angry. Either come out or let me go eat my dinner."

A low, dirty laugh echoed around Diego's room. It sounded like someone scraping burnt branches together. After inhaling a strong scent of sulfur and ash, he cupped his hand over his mouth and nose. His eyes began to burn as a thin mist of smoky residue replaced the still air.

Flaming sapphire pearls fell from the ceiling onto his bed. They sizzled upon making contact, but did not burn the linens. As the seconds ticked by, more and more blazing droplets dripped down onto Diego's bed. Finally, with the entire sheet burning but not ablaze, the laughter returned. It rasped for a few seconds and then silenced itself.

"Hola, Diego," said Magnifico, still nowhere to be found.

"This is quite a show, dragon," said Diego. "Come out and show yourself, or are you afraid?"

A trumpeting roar came from beneath Diego's bed.

Diego froze when the first clawed wing emerged from beneath his bed. He sat in awe of the taut muscles rippling beneath the glossy skin. Magnifico had grown – a lot – since he last saw him at the school library. Suddenly, a second wing appeared, and then, the scaly, horned beak. He heard teeth clattering together as Magnifico pushed his head through the opening, a head as big as half of Diego's body. The wings flared, raking everything off Diego's desk. They flapped once, then twice, and Magnifico's huge body sliced the mattress in two. He sat there amidst the aquamarine fire, resting after his crossing. Then he looked past the sharp horns on his beak at Diego. He grunted, shoving a burst of flame across the room.

Diego tried to brace himself, summoning as much courage as he could. He stared at Magnifico, for he could do nothing else, but he almost pissed his pants when Magnifico turned his scaly eyes in his direction.

"It is about time we met."

"Hola," said Diego, wide eyed but strong.

"Do you know who I am, or why I have come here?"

"You are Magnifico," said Diego. "At least, that's what we've named you."

"Who dares name me?" hissed the dragon.

"A-All of us. I mean, some in my family suggested it, and then Racquel and I..."

"Who?" asked Magnifico, grinding his teeth.

"Racquel, a girl at my school."

"The one who accompanied you when you disposed of me?" Blue, red and yellow flames lapped up from within the black beak. A rancid smoke wafted through gnashing teeth, drifting up to the ceiling.

"Yes," he said, "but she only went to keep me company. It was my idea to get rid of you."

Magnifico lifted his head, roaring and belching smoke so loudly the walls of Diego's bedroom shook. A blast of fire rushed from his mouth, blanketing the ceiling in multicolored flame. Magnifico writhed in pain, visibly shaking.

Diego kept glancing toward the door of his bedroom, wondering when his parents would rescue him from the noise and flames.

"They don't know I'm here."

Diego's head snapped around. He stared at Magnifico with wide eyes. He swore the dragon actually smiled at him.

82

"Yes, mijo, I *can* read your thoughts. Don't worry about anyone finding me here. Our little visit will go completely unnoticed. No one but you will ever know I came here tonight."

Diego believed every word.

"We are bonded," said Magnifico. "You are my Guide, and I am the conduit to your future. Together we will try our best to change the past."

"What do you mean, the past? I'm only eleven years old."

"No, Diego," said Magnifico. "You are wrong. That is why I have come. We must awaken the warrior within."

"What?"

"You are much older than eleven, Diego Ramirez. Do you not feel the fire burning within your blood? Are you not interested in why you have such a brilliant mind? Have you ever told anyone that you've never opened a textbook in your life, and yet your grades are always at the top of every class?"

Diego shivered. *How could Magnifico know these things?*

"I know much about you, my young Guide."

Diego stared at Magnifico. The temperature in the room had risen noticeably. The ceiling would never be the same, and the rest of his room looked no better. His mind raced; he couldn't figure anything out. He decided to get right to the point.

"Magnifico, why are you here, and why me?"

A sinister laugh echoed around the room, and then a low, grumbling growl. "Why you?" asked Magnifico. "Think about your past, your history, and you will discover the answer to your riddle."

"I don't have time for this! Just tell me!"

"Meet me tomorrow morning at three o'clock outside your home and I will show you."

"Midnight," said Diego, "and you'll tell me now."

Magnifico coughed up an acrid cloud of smoke. *The author has chosen correctly after all,* he thought.

"Zapata, Villa, Juarez, do you recognize these names?"

"Of course, but what do they have to do with me?"

Magnifico shot a stream of blue flame from his nostrils. "They *are* you, Diego Ramirez."

CHAPTER SEVENTEEN

"Diego, what's gotten into you?" asked his father. He had watched his son drift lazily to the dinner table. He plopped his rump onto his dining room chair, staring at nothing and saying less. After his mother served his dinner, he stabbed at different areas of the plate like a blind man.

"Usually you're finished eating before your mother and I put our napkins in our laps."

"Yes, mijo," said his mother, "you're worrying us. We've never seen such an attitude at the dinner table."

Diego snapped out of his trance and came to attention. The last thing he needed was his parents snooping around his bedroom. They might find one of Magnifico's smoldering turds in the middle of the floor.

"I'm sorry, Mama, Papa. It's just school. It's getting on my nerves right now. Ever since Magnifico arrived, everyone treats me like some sort of celebrity or something."

"This isn't interfering with your school work, is it mijo?" asked his mother.

"No, it just bugs me."

"I bet all the girls follow you around all day, trying to get the attention of Magnifico's master."

Diego smiled, but his mind was far away. Magnifico had made a strange request before repairing his bedroom and disappearing.

He couldn't understand it, but he would do as he and Magnifico agreed and meet him in the side yard at midnight.

At precisely eleven fifty-nine, long after his parents had turned in for the night, Diego silently slipped his bedcovers away from his body. Without switching on a light, he selected the clothing he had laid out before turning in. He pulled his jeans on, threw a sweatshirt over his head, and stepped into his most comfortable hiking boots. Holding the corner of his desk, he grabbed a heavy coat off the bed. He took one step toward the sliding glass door, tripping over his backpack. He steadied himself, listening for any noise in his parents' bedroom. Finally satisfied that his misstep hadn't disturbed them, he grasped the door handle and slowly slid it across its rail.

Once outside, he exhaled, watching his breath bounce off the glass. Hurrying into his jacket, he stepped lightly around the pool and under his parents' bedroom window.

He carefully grabbed the string connected to the gate lock. His father could reach over the slats and grab the mechanism if he wanted to go out into the yard, but Diego wasn't tall enough to do that yet. He took the string in his fingers, wrapped it around his hand twice, and gave it a soft but steady yank.

The lock gave way with a loud clack that sent a chill down Diego's spine. *Surely my father heard that,* he thought.

No one stirred. No lights flicked on.

Diego pushed through the gate, peering into the darkness of the side yard. He held the wooden door as the tightly coiled spring tried to jerk it closed. He set the lock against the level, leaving it open for his return.

He turned, almost bumping into one of Magnifico's brawny legs. He was gigantic, even bent over by the trees to hide his body.

His huge head whirled on Diego, with a mouth full of spiked teeth that could crush him like a pretzel.

Diego fell back a few steps, shaken by Magnifico's immense size. He stumbled into his mother's favorite rose bushes. Trying to steady himself, he grabbed a branch full of fat thorns. He couldn't help himself, he cried out, trying to yank his hand away, but the dense thorns held it fast. He screamed, the pain was that great, finally ripping his hand away from the bush.

Lights flicked on in his parents' bedroom. The sliding glass door near the pool slid back. It slammed against the end of the track and Diego's father came outside demanding to know who dared enter their yard.

"Diego," said Magnifico. "We must leave, *now.*"

"Leave?" he asked. "And go where?"

"By all the mystical powers, Diego, stop ranting and climb aboard my back. I have minimal powers of invisibility when I grow to this size. Now get on my back and hold on!"

The look in Magnifico's eyes convinced him. He ran up the long tail, grabbing scales and horns as he went. Before he even reached Magnifico's shoulders, the dragon lifted his great body from the grassy yard. Diego nearly fell off, but he found a huge spike right by the dragon's muscular shoulders. He wrapped his arms around it.

Magnifico took one mighty jump, pushing his body skyward. His leathery wings pumped wildly, driving huge gusts of air back toward the ground. With each mighty pull, he drove his massive body toward the stars.

He didn't look around to see if Diego had accompanied him. He expected his guide to remember how to fly a dragon. *So what if it'd been years since the last time they had flown together,* he thought as he climbed into the night sky.

With trembling knees, Diego knelt on Magnifico's shoulders. The tough, scaly skin wasn't exactly comfortable, but somehow his body blended in with the rippling muscles and bony bulges on Magnifico's back. The horn Diego clutched served two purposes; it kept him from falling off and it gave him shelter from the howling winds.

Neighborhoods disappeared underneath them as they flew along to who knew where. Diego's eyes watered, his hair flew about, and his jacket flapped wildly. Even if he wanted to, he wouldn't be able to say anything to his monstrous friend, so he made himself as comfortable as he could. He half knelt, half sat next to the grizzled horn, holding on tighter with every twist and turn.

With a tempered roar, Magnifico banked sharply over a busy highway. Diego pushed hard with his feet, trying to stay in position as the dragon's body leaned hard to the left. He couldn't help but look down at the cars and people. *They must not be able to see us*, he thought, *Magnifico's skin is so dark, he must look like a drifting shadow or cloud in the night sky.*

Magnifico coasted along on a night breeze, leaving the residential area behind him. After a few pulls of his wings, his nostrils began to flare. He inhaled the scent of a thousand earthly delights, all rotting together in the same stinking heap. He smelled rather than saw their destination. He flew lower, descending into a huge industrial site. They glided over a dump, a mining operation, and a cement production facility. Magnifico roared, identifying himself to whoever might be unfortunate enough to encounter them.

Maybe he's telling someone we're here, thought Diego. He couldn't imagine any other reason for their journey. Magnifico was far too grand to hang out at a dump when he wasn't scaring the pants off of elementary school students.

Before Diego could ready himself, Magnifico dove straight for the mining field. Diego nearly rolled off his shoulders and once again found himself clinging to the horn.

"Not so fast!" he yelled.

Diego watched the ground rushing toward him with such speed he almost closed his eyes and jumped. At the last second, Magnifico flicked his wings, sending the two of them soaring over the site and upward again. He dipped his other wing, making one final pass so he could inspect the grounds. Then he landed lightly, barely jostling his guide.

Diego half slid, half fell from Magnifico's back. He landed in a crouch, staring at the unbelievable sight before him. Magnifico had grown even larger during the flight from his house to wherever they had landed. His tail alone looked like it was fifty feet long. The huge head seemed as big as a railroad car. The body looked longer than a whale's.

Diego looked at the mining machinery. He saw a loading mechanism for the cement and a huge crane sitting beside it. Magnifico dwarfed both of them. If he wanted, he could reduce them to nothing but a pile of twisted metal.

"So, Guide," came the low, guttural voice that sounded more like an earthquake than an animal. "Did you enjoy your flight?"

Magnifico didn't seem to be paying attention to Diego, but nonetheless the question had been asked.

"Scary, but fun," he said.

A sputter of laughter emerged from where the dragon had been grooming his scales. Towering puffs of sulfur laden soot shot forward from his nose. "You've found the right one, Nathan, his honesty gives him away."

Diego whipped around, looking for the strange man who had

changed his life. He caught sight of him walking toward Magnifico as if he were approaching a harmless dog. He had a curious smile on his face.

"Good evening, Diego," he said, bowing slightly.

"His name is Guide," rumbled Magnifico.

"What the hell's going on," asked Diego. "Tell me now or take me home."

The rumbling began anew, this time with an impatient tone.

"You will go home, Diego," said Sullivan. "It might seem as though your life will never be the same, but I promise you, it will."

"Are you loco? Look at what's standing behind me!"

Magnifico raised his head, peeling his lips back into a gristly smile.

"Diego?" asked Sullivan, "has our big friend said anything to you about who you are, or why I gave you the statue at your school?"

"He was talking crazy, loco, like I was the descendant of a high priest of Toltec or something."

"That is *not* what I said!" shouted Magnifico. The expansive grounds of the mining operation trembled as Magnifico's voice echoed thunderously. His massive tail slid across the length of his body as he stood on all fours and rose up to the sky. He stood taller than a five-story building, ten tons of pissed off dragon.

"Easy, my friend," said Sullivan. "We don't need the police coming down on us. As dark as your skin may be, a voice that sounds like a sonic boom will attract everyone within five miles."

Magnifico settled down. "My apologies," he said softly, looking first at Sullivan and then at Diego. "I told him exactly who he is. He could at least have the decency to quote me correctly."

"Diego?" asked Sullivan.

"It doesn't make sense. How can it be?"

Diego felt Sullivan's eyes boring into him. He looked over at Magnifico and saw an unblinking eye gazing at him. The blood red iris shone brightly even in the dark of night.

"No, it just can't be. I'm not your holy savior no matter what you think."

A soft but menacing snarl worked its way through Magnifico's throat. Sullivan held his hand up to the dragon, silently asking him to give Diego a little more time.

"We all have trouble accepting our destiny," he said. "I admit we've located you at a young age, but that doesn't alter anything Magnifico told you. The blood of the great warriors and statesmen of your ancestry burns within you, Diego."

"It's not possible. Zapata and Villa lived at the same time. If I *am* them, then why didn't they all live in different times in history?"

Magnifico burped a rolling ball of smoky fire. Diego could tell he was becoming annoyed. *Dragons must not be able to display the same tolerance as humans,* he thought. *In fact, they probably couldn't keep calm about anything.*

The beast turned his attention to Diego. "Do you believe the ways of your world to be the ways of all worlds? Perhaps I am mistaken and we have found the wrong boy. A guide would understand parallel existence."

Sullivan tilted his head toward Magnifico. "He is eleven years old, my friend. Let's try and show him a little patience."

Diego stood quietly as Magnifico and Sullivan exchanged comments. The scenery began shifting in front of his eyes. He remembered racing through the desert with Zapata's men, and witnessing the discussion between the leaders of his country. He thought of the way Juarez had stared him down in that room, asking him what they should do – fight or talk. He felt a strange blend of strength and purpose flooding his mind.

Magnifico no longer looked like an enormous, terrifying monster. Sullivan lost the appearance of a stranger. In fact, he looked like an old friend. In a matter of a few breaths, everything became clear. He knew exactly who Sullivan was, how many times he'd seen him in the past, and under what circumstances.

Zapata, Villa and Juarez. He felt the blood of all of them coursing through his veins. He listened to their voices welcoming him, speaking to him as brothers. A wave of mystical recognition swept over Diego. He felt weak at the knees with the discovery of his identity. It wasn't every day a sixth grade boy found out he might be on a collision course with an unknown destiny.

"I-I understand now," he said. He glanced at Sullivan before staring at Magnifico. "I'm sorry, I've been stupid. Forgive me."

An entirely different sound poured out from Magnifico's belly. Diego smiled. Sullivan laughed. The ferocious dragon was actually purring, if one could call it that.

"It is good to finally see you again, old friend," he said, smoke curling up through his teeth. "It has been too long, Guide."

"Si," said Diego. "Much too long."

"You have work to do, Diego, and we have much planning to attend to," said Sullivan. "I'm afraid you have many such days ahead. The role of a guide will demand far more of you than you can imagine."

"I figured," said the young boy. "But I'm not afraid anymore. I guess the world's bigger than me and my problems."

Magnifico smiled broadly. "Nathan, you may report back to the high council that the guide has been found and he is ready to undertake his mission."

"I'm proud of you, Diego," said Sullivan. "We're both very pleased. Now, off with you. Magnifico must take you home before the sun peeks over the eastern horizon."

"How will you get home?" asked Diego.

"The usual way," said Sullivan with a sly wink.

"Come, Diego," said Magnifico. He flattened out his left wing, giving his guide an easy path to his perch.

"Until we meet again, Nathan," said Magnifico.

Sullivan had already started walking across the grainy grounds of the mining operation. Without turning, he lifted one arm and gave a brief wave. Then, right before Diego's eyes, he vanished.

CHAPTER EIGHTEEN

Before Diego could react, he felt Magnifico's bulk stirring beneath him. He located the horn on the ridge of Magnifico's neck, knelt, and hung on. He watched the wings flailing against the air as they scrambled into the dark sky.

In minutes, they were sailing over the city, high enough so they wouldn't be seen, but low enough for Diego to see the buildings they passed. He glanced at block after empty block, looking for any kind of movement or signs of life. With the early hour, few people walked along the filthy, untidy streets.

Diego almost put his head down to rest, when suddenly he saw someone familiar. He leaned over Magnifico's neck as much as he could to get a better view. *Esteban! What's he doing down here? Is he loco?* He scrambled forward a little and yelled into Magnifico's ear.

"My brother's down there. I think he might be in trouble."

"Your brother, the one who pushes you around and is disrespectful to your parents?"

"He's my brother. If he's in trouble I want to help him. Let's go down there."

"Who are you to order *me* around?"

"I'm the guide, remember? Now move it."

Magnifico smiled as he banked into a wide turn. He reversed course as he dropped toward the ground.

"Come in a block behind them. I don't want you to be seen."

"I assure you, Guide, I will not be seen, other than by you, of course."

Magnifico floated down to the street. He banked left and right, finally landing in an alley behind the building where Diego had seen Esteban. As he descended into the trash-strewn passage, he altered his shape so his wings would fit between the structures. After landing, he quickly reduced his size until he became the statue Diego had won a few weeks prior at his school.

What am I supposed to do with this, thought Diego. *What if I need help?* He grabbed the statue and ran to the sidewalk. As he approached the street corner he heard men arguing. There were many voices, but the one that stood out came from his brother.

Diego ran around the building, stopping suddenly in front of six tough looking men from the neighborhood. They stared back, shocked.

"Diego?" asked Esteban. "What the hell are you doing in the city?"

"I can't tell you, but I saw you here with these other guys and I wanted to make sure you were all right."

The men confronting Esteban burst out laughing. Esteban was the only one without a smile on his face. He knew these men from hanging around the city. He also knew Diego had made a terrible mistake by coming to help him.

"Get lost, poquito, before one of us hurts you."

"If I were you guys," said Diego, "I'd get out of here fast."

"Diego," warned Esteban. He shook his head, signaling for his brother to stop speaking.

One of the men walked toward Diego, who stood his ground. The man slapped him across the face, hard. "Go on, puto, or you're going to get hurt."

"Do what he says, Diego," said Esteban.

"Yeah, do what he says, said another man. "Vamanos, right now and maybe we won't--hey, what's that you're holding, little niño?"

The man had seen Magnifico.

Obviously drunk, he stormed up to Diego and grabbed the statue by the neck. He yanked hard, twice, but Diego would not let his prize go that easily.

"Leave him alone, asshole," yelled Esteban. "He's just a kid."

"You shut your face," said the leader of the men. "You'll be lucky if you ever see home again."

The man struggling for the statue kicked Diego in the stomach and wrenched Magnifico away from him. He ignored the young man fighting for breath on the sidewalk as he glanced at his prize. After a minute, he swore bitterly and threw the statue toward the alley.

"Stupid Tijuana plaster mold," he said. "It isn't worth a dime. I don't know why the kid was fighting so hard for it, anyway."

Diego got to his knees, coughing. Spittle and blood dripped from his mouth.

The man who had kicked him walked up and slapped him on the left side of his face. Diego cried out.

"Dumb ass," said the man.

Suddenly, from deep within the confines of the alley came a menacing snarl.

"What the hell was that?" asked another man.

"Pinche perro, that's all," said the one who had slapped Diego.

"That ain't no dog."

Diego looked up and called out. "Run away while you can. He's right, it isn't a dog."

The men held their ground.

A large eucalyptus tree by the end of the alley started shaking like a twig in a tornado. With a resounding crack, the heavy trunk snapped in two. The tree toppled over into the street like a drunken giant.

"Go, now!" warned Diego.

A blast of white-hot flame poured out from the depths of the alley, consuming the tree in a flash of brilliant fire. It lay sizzling on the street, a crackling ember. A thunderous roar shattered plate glass windows for two blocks in both directions.

Magnifico's horned head, blacker than the night it occupied, shot forward from the alley. The spiked nose collided with two cars parked by the sidewalk, shoving them to the opposite side of the street. The cars crashed against each other before colliding with a storefront. They took out everything in their path - rusty parking meters, discolored trashcans, even the recently planted flower basins.

The men on the sidewalk forgot all about Diego and Esteban. When Magnifico whipped his head around to face them, their wide eyes and shaking knees told them everything they needed to know. They had been warned, they chose to ignore it, and now an unimaginable horror pounded down the sidewalk toward them, snarling its disapproval.

Magnifico exploded from the alley, crushing the sidewalk beneath his talons as he stormed over to the man who had beaten Diego.

"Who are *you* to assault the guide of the greatest dragon that ever lived?"

The man opened his mouth but nothing came out. He took a step backward. Magnifico bared his teeth and growled again.

"Apologize or you'll look worse than that tree!"

"S-Sorry," said the man. "I-I'm s-sorry." His legs trembled as the scaly neck unraveled, pushing the dragon's head backward. He felt the wind rushing past him as Magnifico drew in a belly full of oxygen. He saw the blood-red eyes narrow."

"Run!" yelled Diego. "Run, you idiots!"

The man needed no further urging. Fueled by panic and adrenaline, he turned and tore down the street. Two others followed. Magnifico pressed his spiked head forward. With a mighty exhale, he spat out three brilliant streams of fire. The flames scorched the sidewalk, catching the running figures an instant later. Magnifico ordered the fire to consume them. Seconds later it looked as if they never existed.

"Magnifico!" said Diego. "What have you done?"

A shot rang out. Diego whipped around. The leader of the men held a gun. A lazy wisp of smoke curled away from the barrel. Magnifico glanced at an insignificant scratch on one of his scales.

Three things happened at once. Diego yelled at Magnifico, the man with the gun put Diego in a headlock with his free hand, and Esteban tried his best to wrestle the gun away.

Magnifico bared his jagged teeth, fire sizzling past his lips. "Those such as you do not deserve a place among civilized people," he snarled.

The dragon blinked his eyes once. The man with the gun released Diego and watched the ground sail away under his feet. He dropped the gun as he soared higher and higher into the sky. The last image he saw was Diego and his brother Esteban, someone he would surely never bother again.

Diego watched the confused man shoot up into the sky. Farther and farther he went, until neither Diego nor his brother could see him.

"Magnifico," Diego yelled. "Make them come back, all of them, now!"

The massive head whirled around, facing Diego. Esteban backed away several steps, wondering how his younger brother could stand his ground against the dragon.

"You would have your world populated by such uncivilized cretins?"

"It is not up to me, or you," yelled Diego. "Bring them back!"

"Is this truly what you wish?"

"I said now!" ordered Diego.

Magnifico blasted a heavy cloud of smoke from his lungs. "Once the magic has been invoked, it is rarely reclaimed. Those who threaten the journey suffer the consequences. However, since you are the guide, I will respect your wishes."

Esteban backtracked toward the alley. He stepped toward the cobbled street until Magnifico caught sight of his movements.

"And what about you?" he snarled. "Have you nothing better to do than endanger yourself and your brother?"

Esteban stood his ground, seriously considering whether he should drink again in the future. Whatever it was, his mind couldn't accept that it was real. Huge dragons from storybooks didn't just appear out of nowhere.

"*Well?*" asked Magnifico, growling, his scales gleaming.

"Y-you didn't have to come here," said Esteban, stammering as he looked from the dragon to Diego and back to the dragon again. "I would have been fine without you, both of you."

Magnifico scoffed. A putrid fire drooled over his bottom teeth. He wondered if Sullivan's choice of journeys made sense any longer. He glanced at Diego as he watched the dawn approaching.

"Go home," he said to Esteban, "Stay away from the city at

night, if that's at all possible. We might not be around the next time you find yourself facing a beating."

"Esteban," said Diego. "Forget what you saw. I can't explain everything that's happening because I don't really understand it myself."

Diego's brother looked at Magnifico one last time.

"Thanks, Diego," he said. "I owe you one." He ran off, but before leaving, he glanced over at Magnifico. "You, too, big boy, gracias."

"Denada, estupido," snarled Magnifico.

CHAPTER NINETEEN

Diego woke the next morning exhausted. After Magnifico returned him to his home, he had crashed in his bed for a little over thirty minutes before his father knocked on his door.

"Mijo?" he asked, tapping lightly. "Time to get up, the bus for school leaves in forty minutes."

Diego rubbed his eyes hard. He yawned, stretching his jaws as wide as they would go. Afterward, he stumbled into the bathroom.

He showered, dressed, and ran down the hall toward the kitchen. Just before he reached the doorway, he heard his mother's voice rising with disbelief.

"Do you believe this story in the paper?" she asked of her husband. "A fire comes out of nowhere, burning a sidewalk in the downtown area to nothing."

Diego stood silently outside of the kitchen, listening to his parents' exchange.

"How did the fire start?" his father asked.

"An explosion of some sort, so they say. Apparently it destroyed two cars, three store fronts and *melted* a ring of planters in front of the bicycle racks."

"Melted?" asked his father.

"Same as the sidewalk. The plants burned away to nothing. The planters look like a decoration in a Dr. Seuss book."

"Strange. Did they catch anyone?"

"Only a group of boys from that club downtown, but they didn't actually catch them. The boys ran to the police station claiming a giant dragon attacked them in front of the liquor store."

"What?" asked his father, "they must be loco!"

"Apparently the police think so. They hauled them into some interrogation rooms, asking them all sorts of questions."

"How many?"

"Three, it says here, but it also says the police brought in another three boys from the same club. The strange thing is they all have identical stories. They agree with each other, almost perfectly. You wouldn't believe what they're saying."

"Try me," said Diego's father.

"They said a young boy appeared out of nowhere in the middle of the night. He was carrying a dragon statue in his hand."

Diego's blood ran cold. He stood as quietly as he could.

"There was a fight and that's when the boys from the club claim they saw the dragon for the first time. A black dragon, they said, bigger than a three story house."

"A boy, with a statue?" asked Alvaro.

Diego considered running back down to his room and escaping through the sliding glass door by the pool. He knew his mother would catch him, though. She could hear anything, smell anything, and see everything. The best thing to do would be to walk into the kitchen as if he didn't hear anything.

He passed through the door while pretending to rub sleep from his eyes. He swept his right hand through his hair, and then pulled up his uniform slacks with both hands.

"Diego Ramirez," said his mother sternly. "Tie those shoelaces before you trip over one and knock yourself out."

Diego looked up sheepishly at his father as he knelt down to do his mother's bidding. He heard her pick up the newspaper and snap the fold crisply. She pretended to read the article while waiting for Diego to stand up.

"Did you sleep well last night, mijo?" she asked.

"Okay. I had some weird dreams, but they didn't wake me up or anything. Did you sleep well, Mama?"

"As well as anyone could sleep with their son out until all hours of the night."

Diego's body twitched the tiniest bit, enough for his mother to see. "Are you loco, Mama? I was in my room all night, like I said."

"Watch what you say to your mother, Diego," warned his father, "you know very well we don't talk like that in this house."

"Sorry, Papa, I'm sorry, Mama."

His mother refused to be placated. "Look at this newspaper," she said. "Can you imagine how I felt when I read about these lunatics telling a story about a young boy and a dragon in the city, and in the early hours of the morning?"

"I'm sorry you're scared, Mama, but I swear, I was in my room all night. Magnifico sat on my desk the whole time, watching over me."

Diego's mother stared at him, giving him the look no boy ever wants to see. His father slid his chair back noisily, slamming it against the wall.

Diego snapped his eyes toward his father. He didn't like the look he saw there, either. He knew he'd be getting a lecture on the way to school.

"You don't believe any of that, do you, Mama?" he asked as he slid into his seat at the table. "You really think I was running around downtown last night with my statue and that I made him come to life so he could chase away the bad guys?"

"I'm not sure what to think. Ever since Señor Sullivan, gentleman though he may be, gave you that dragon statue, all kinds of strange things have been happening."

"Maybe we should invite him to dinner again," said Alvaro. "I have some questions I'd like to ask him."

"You can't!" said Diego.

"What do you mean, we can't?" asked Alejandra.

"H-He's gone. In another country, I think."

"And how would you know that, Diego Ramirez?"

Diego thought quickly. "Mrs. Coble told us. He went to visit other schools and sign books."

"If one of my children might be in danger," said his mother, "I don't care where he is. If he can't visit our home, then we'll have to track him down by cell phone."

Diego felt trapped. He knew what would come next.

"Diego," his father said. "Tell Mrs. Coble to call me at work today. I want to see if I can find Señor Sullivan."

"Si, Papa." Diego wolfed down his breakfast, and after placing his dish, glass, and silverware in the dishwasher he walked briskly toward the hallway.

"Mijo," said his father. "Aren't you forgetting something?"

Diego froze for a moment. He didn't understand. Then he looked back at the kitchen table. He ran around the table and pushed his chair in. Then he reversed course and headed for the hallway again.

"Bus leaves in five minutes," said his father.

Diego heard his cell phone humming in his bedroom. He ran down the hallway and darted into his room. He saw his cell phone squirming in a loose semicircle by the penholder on his desk. He walked over, flipped it open, and saw Racquel's name flashing in the screen.

"Diego, was that you outside in the middle of the night? Did you have Magnifico with you?"

"Not now, Racquel," he said quietly. "I'll talk to you about it at school."

"Just say yes or no, Diego, I can't stand thinking about it. I can't believe what my father said when he was reading the paper."

"My Dad's coming down the hall. I'll see you at school, Racquel. I promise we'll talk about it then."

"First thing," she snapped. "Wait for me outside of the school office."

"Okay, mijo," said Diego's father. "Off you go, and don't forget to get Mr. Sullivan's phone number."

"Okay, Papa, I promise." Diego started to swing the door shut, but his father held out a strong, tanned arm.

"Is that Racquel running over to meet you? She's muy bonita, that one, I'd be proud if you'd invite her and her parents over for dinner some weekend."

"Adios, Papa," said Diego, leaning into the door to slam it shut.

Racquel wasn't the only one running toward Diego. It looked like half the student body was streaming through the gates toward his father's truck. Diego tried to grab Racquel and dodge the crowd, but excited students were swarming toward them from all directions.

"Diego, where is Magnifico?" several of them asked at once.

"Was he downtown last night? Were you with him? Why didn't you tell us he was a real dragon?"

Frustrated and scared, Diego shook his head each time one of his fellow students shouted a question at him. He didn't know what to do, and when the first bell rang, he silently thanked his creator for the interruption.

"Let's get out of here," he yelled into Racquel's ear. He saw her briskly nod her head and then lean toward his right ear.

"C'mon," she whispered, "I know a place where we can be alone."

They hurried down the main hallway, their backpacks bouncing on their backs as they ran. Two teachers and a vice principal admonished them, advising them to slow down or face detention after school. Racquel flashed her brilliant smile as they sped by, taking Diego to the end of the corridor. She turned right, ducking into the first door she passed. She dragged Diego through the theater arts auditorium until they were alone behind a large, partially constructed set.

They squatted down, trying to slow their breathing as they listened for the sounds of other students in the theater. After a few tense seconds, Racquel looked up at Diego. Even though they were taking a big chance by not reporting to their classrooms, Diego nearly lost it when he looked at her in the dimly lit room. If she hadn't started talking right away, he might have flopped over and fainted right in front of her.

"Diego," she said a little too loudly. "Was that you last night in the city?"

He just stared at her, lost in his first schoolboy crush.

"Tell me," she said a little more forcefully. "Was it Magnifico my father told me about this morning?"

"Yes," he said, finally tearing himself away from her radiant eyes. "Yes, Racquel, it was him. I was with him last night. He saved my brother from a bad situation. I swear he gets more powerful every time he comes alive."

"Why is he here? What does he want with you?"

Diego decided not to tell Racquel the whole story, so he told a little fib. "I don't know everything, he hasn't said much about me yet."

"He talks to you?" asked Racquel excitedly.

She also kept a secret. It had to do with Diego's journey, but she decided to keep it to herself for the time being. If she discovered more about Magnifico, perhaps she would tell him.

Damn, thought Diego. *I shouldn't have said that.*

"What has he said so far? Oh, I can't believe this is happening to us!"

"Not much. He keeps mumbling something about a great mission or something stupid like that."

"Stupid? Are you loco? Do you know how many kids all over the world would want to be in your place?"

"Racquel, I…"

"Yes, what is it?"

"You can't say anything to anyone, I mean about Magnifico. Do you understand?"

"All right, Diego, I won't, on one condition."

"What's that?" asked Diego.

"That you tell me everything that happens with Magnifico from now on. And I mean everything."

"Racquel!"

"Promise me or I swear I'll run down the hall right now screaming all about you and Magnifico."

"Okay, I promise," said Diego. "Besides, it doesn't matter anyway."

"What's that supposed to mean?"

"It means you'll probably find out anyway."

"Why?" asked Racquel.

"Magnifico's talked about you a few times. I think you might be involved somehow."

"Me? Involved in what?"

"I'm not sure, Racquel. Like I told you, he hasn't said much. Your name came up a couple of times, that's all, especially when Mr. Sullivan showed up." As soon as he mentioned the mysterious writer, Diego cringed. *Estupido! Why did I mention him!*

"You've seen him again?" *This gets better every second,* she thought.

The final bell for first period rang. Diego gathered his backpack, expecting Racquel to do the same, but she seemed too excited to leave. She leaned forward on her knees, forgetting all about the fact that they were at school and about to be called to the office for truancy.

"What did he say?" she asked. "Do I get to meet Magnifico?"

Diego stood, shouldered his backpack and motioned to Racquel. "We better get to our first class. Right now I need more attention about as much as I need Magnifico to burn down my room again."

"Isn't this incredible?" asked Racquel. She jumped up and threw her backpack over her shoulder. Before Diego could react, she surprised him with a quick peck on the cheek before running into the main room and out the door.

Even after she'd left Diego could sense the sweet smell of her hair. *Great,* he thought, *first, I become friends with un dragón gigante and now a girl I've had a crush on for a year decides she likes me!*

He peered around the back wall of the set into the theater. He saw no one there, so he hustled through the room and out the door. He hadn't gotten three steps before a security guard yelled out his name.

"Diego! How come you're not in class?"

Diego turned and breathed a sigh of relief. It was Hector, the nicest of all the guards. "I'm sorry, sir, I lost track of time. I'm going to class right now."

"It wouldn't have anything to do with a certain young lady at this school, now would it?"

He could do nothing but smile. "We were talking, and..."

"Okay, mijo, come along with me. I'll walk you to class. If we see anyone, though, you'll have to come with me to the principal's office. It's my job, mijo, you understand, don't you?"

"Si, I understand," said Diego. "I wouldn't want to get you in any trouble. You're the gordo contento, the nice one."

Hector smiled. "You mean the happy, fat one, huh?"

As the words left Hector's mouth, a teacher stepped out of her classroom and into the hallway. "Got another one, eh, Hector?"

"Yes, Ma'am, caught him by the theater."

Hector looked down at his little charge and shrugged his shoulders. The tiniest smile spread from the corners of his mouth, also at the crease in his eyes. One of his huge arms swept toward Diego, guiding the young man in the direction of his doom.

CHAPTER TWENTY

"Are we certain we're not moving too fast?" asked Sullivan. "He doesn't seem ready. Anything could have happened in the city last night. You were lucky to get away with what you did."

Magnifico snarled. He felt tempted to blast Sullivan with a wave of fire that would leave nothing but a pile of ashes. "No one has any idea of the true origin of last night's skirmish. The men I disposed of are all alive and well. No doubt, Diego already heard this from someone today. No permanent damage has been done."

"And Diego's brother, Esteban?"

An acrid smoke wafted up from both sides of the dragon's upper jaw. "Yes, he is a problem. No doubt he has presented his version of the story all over the city by now."

"But who would believe him?"

"Who would believe the wildest tale one could tell?" asked Magnifico, "Only those who seek answers from falsehoods. Your species has developed a tendency toward the absurd, Nathan."

"This is not the time to ridicule each other, dragon. We have a serious problem before us. I, for one, do not think Diego is ready to assume his responsibilities."

"The path has been prepared," growled Magnifico. "After centuries, we have located the true guide. Neither you nor I can change who he is, or what he must accomplish for his people."

"And if he fails?"

"Then he fails," answered the dragon. "Although, I believe he will not. There is strength in him, you see it as well as I."

"I see recklessness as well."

"He is an eleven year-old-boy, Nathan. What were you doing at that tender age, I wonder?"

Sullivan looked up at Magnifico. He grinned, and then stretched his face into a wide smile. The laughter that followed caused the dragon to rear back in mild misunderstanding.

Sullivan, looking much less strained after his fit of hilarity, turned around and leaned against the soft scales on Magnifico's belly. "Yes," he said, breathing heavily, "I suppose our little guide has quite a bit more on his plate than he can handle."

"After tonight's journey," said Magnifico, "he will have all he can handle and more."

CHAPTER TWENTY-ONE

Though exhausted, Diego slept restlessly that night. Bizarre dreams invaded his thoughts.

In one, he saw a sky filled with so many stars he felt he could touch them. Then Marisol's face came into view. It floated among the stars like another moon, the beautiful eyes beckoning Diego to rise up and follow her.

Her left hand appeared from within a circle of light. Stretching toward him, the fingers expanded as the palm turned up.

A voice called out from the heavens. "Come with me, Diego. I wish to show you something."

At first Diego wouldn't respond. He shuddered at the thought of touching the hand and having it change into a clawed extension of some savage monster from Magnifico's world. Finally, as he looked into Marisol's hypnotic eyes, he reached out to her.

When their fingers met he felt the ground falling away. A light wind washed over his face as Marisol pulled him toward the heavens. She looked back, gently checking on her passenger's safety.

Within seconds, Marisol and Diego were flying beneath a blanket of brilliant stars. She smiled when she saw his face fill with wonder. Noticing that his nerves had finally calmed, she increased her pace, soaring like an angel in the heavens.

Holding Marisol's hand tightly, Diego looked all around him. He barely noticed the cities far below them. *Wherever we are,* he thought, *we're a long way from home.*

He watched as a passenger jet passed underneath them on its way to an airport cradled close to the sea. *San Diego*, he thought. His father had taken the family there more than once. They had even flown from there to Hawaii one year. Diego looked closely, as much as he could from such a height.

Marisol veered left, away from the approaching ocean. Diego felt a roller coaster sensation as his escort dropped closer to the city. The two travelers passed many of the communities in San Diego, heading farther out into East County. At their lower altitude Diego could see things like buildings, cars, and people. He could just make out the telltale sounds of the cities.

Soon the buildings faded away as Marisol and Diego soared onward toward the east. A lonely desert lay below them, swathed in lazy dunes and rambling scrub brush. Diego looked in every direction but saw nothing except a desolate land.

The air in the sky cooled, raising goose bumps on Diego's arms. Marisol dropped again, leaving them slightly more than a few hundred yards above the desert floor.

Suddenly, Diego saw tears falling from Marisol's eyes. She began to weep openly, and her sobs cut into his heart like a scalpel.

"Marisol," he asked, "what is it, what do you see?"

Saying nothing, the young woman continued to cry as she looked down upon the sandy floor beneath her.

"What do you see?" asked Diego again. He looked below them, but couldn't spot anything that might bring about the sadness Marisol expressed.

They traveled onward, over miles of scrub-strewn desert. Marisol wiped her eyes with her free hand, trying to compose herself. Each time she did, a new wave of tears emerged.

Diego watched her head moving back and forth as they continued flying east through the desert. Trying to focus on her line of sight, he peered down to the sand. He hoped to locate exactly what it was she saw.

Suddenly, the sand shifted below him. He couldn't make it out completely, but it did look as though some form had emerged from the floor of the desert. Diego didn't know what it was, but it moved along the sand at a slow, measured rate.

He strained his eyes, but he couldn't identify the shapes wandering in the desert. He could tell one thing, though. There were hundreds of them, whatever they were, maybe even thousands. The strange hacienda of his vision returned. He remembered the men discussing whether to attack or negotiate. Was there some connection? Would his choice mean life or death for so many beings?

Marisol began rising into the sky. Diego tugged hard on her hand, trying desperately to get her to reverse course. He couldn't allow her to take him away after getting so close to discovering her secret.

As she pulled him higher, he strained to see the forms far below him. They began to take shape, but they were too distant for Diego to recognize.

In a fit of immaturity, he yanked his hand away from her grip. He immediately fell toward earth, gaining speed every second. He screamed for Marisol to save him, but she continued on her path toward the heavens. As she soared farther into the sky, he saw her body begin to vanish. She became one with the stars, and as she disappeared, she called down to him.

"Do not forget what you saw here, hermano menor."

Diego hesitated one moment before turning his body so he

could face the ground. In seconds, he would be smashed to bits. He closed his eyes, waiting for the horrible smack as his body slammed against the hard ground of the desert.

Just then, a powerful claw emerged from nowhere and wrapped itself around Diego's body. As surprised and shocked as he felt, he knew to whom it belonged.

"Got you," rumbled Magnifico.

Diego cried out in pain as the huge claw gripped his body. "Would you sacrifice your life to discover the secret of the desert? Does such a desolate place hold a strange fascination for you? Do you have any idea what squirmed below you in the hard crusted dirt and brush?"

Magnifico squeezed even harder. "Would you give the lives of everyone you know to solve a riddle when you haven't even heard the question? You disappoint me, Guide!"

Magnifico opened his massive jaws. Diego saw the flames shooting forth from the pit of the dragon's lungs, a fire so hot that it burned Magnifico's mouth as it poured out from his throat.

The flames exploded toward Diego, wrapping him in a fiery cocoon. He screamed, but Magnifico kept the inferno focused on his small companion, cranking up the heat to impossible degrees. Diego felt his skin, muscles, and bones withering away to nothing.

An instant later, the two of them appeared in the side yard of Diego's home. Like a pair of cornstalks, Magnifico and Diego silently pushed up through the ground next to each other. Diego looked at the giant dragon just in time to see him curdling the flames into his mouth with his scarred, smoky tongue.

He checked his body quickly. He expected to feel crusted clothing and charred skin wherever he placed his hands, but instead, he felt nothing out of the ordinary. He touched his hair, his face, and then stared at his hands in disbelief.

He had felt the skin melting away from his body. He had known death was near. He'd been reduced to a smoking shell of a boy with only a single thought left in his fading mind.

"Diego?" called Alvaro. "Mijo? Where are you, mijo?"

Magnifico turned, but he had no time to disappear before Diego's father rounded the far end of the ivy that covered their home's east wall.

"Diego!" said Alvaro, peeking around the dense plants. He looked worried and irritated. "Qué pasa? What are you doing out here? Don't you know your mother is frantically searching for you?"

Diego nearly fainted at the sight of his father. Magnifico hadn't been able to shrink to his smaller size, so he quickly pushed his enormous body against the ivy and stayed as still as possible. He looked like a stone dragon in a Japanese garden, although a very large one. Diego flicked his eyes to Magnifico's scales and then quickly back to his father.

"I-I thought I heard Esteban," he said, stammering. "I could have sworn I heard him by the pool, calling through my door. He sounded hurt so I pulled on some clothes and came out to see."

"What clothes?" asked his father.

Diego started to answer when he suddenly realized he was standing in the yard in his underwear. The cold breeze introduced itself to his naked body. He hadn't realized how freezing it was until his father's last comment.

"I-I must have forgotten to put them on."

"Mijo?" asked Alvaro.

"I heard him. He was out here. I swear."

"Let's go back inside. I'm sure your mother will be thankful to know you're okay."

Diego sighed. At last he could go inside and jump into his warm bed. He fell in behind his father, glancing over at Magnifico one last time.

He saw the giant dragon scrunching his head into his body. His massive face contorted, wrinkling as much as the scales could possibly allow. The eyes closed tightly, and his huge, spiked nostrils twitched as if someone held a ticklish feather under the sensitive skin.

He was about to sneeze!

The spasm burst deep within Magnifico's belly. The harder he tried to keep the explosion from traveling to his nose, the more powerful and anxious it became. When it finally rumbled past his throat and burst from his nostrils, the blast had the power of an earthquake.

The thunderous roar from Magnifico's nose woke everyone within five blocks. Lights turned on in every home on Diego's street. Car alarms blared from dozens of vehicles.

Magnifico's supersonic sneeze knocked Diego and his father out cold. Diego awoke with his head in his mother's grip, her hand slapping him lightly on the cheek. He rolled his head over and looked at his father. He hadn't awakened yet, which alarmed Diego, but within seconds he saw him stir. His barrel chest heaved once before rising up and down evenly.

"Mi esposo," cried Alejandra. As soon as she felt certain her son had survived, she tended to her love. "Thank the Blessed Mother," she cooed, as her husband propped himself up on one elbow.

"Ohhh," mumbled Diego's father. "What happened? Mi cabesa, ohhh."

"Lie back down, Alvaro," said Diego's mother. "The medical teams will be here shortly." She looked back to Diego, who had sat up and crossed his legs. Her young son looked dazed but uninjured. He gazed around the neighborhood numbly, watching all the people exit their homes.

Everyone was talking about the explosion. As a swarm of emergency vehicles descended upon the area, Diego raised his eyes to the sky. Everybody around him focused intently on each other, seeing to the goodwill of their friends and neighbors. Diego scanned the sky nonetheless.

After a few seconds, he spotted him, the dark dragon that almost destroyed his home just by sneezing. Silently, Magnifico rose farther into the sky, until he finally turned downwind, letting the currents hold him aloft as he rested.

"Look at that!" said Diego's father. "The whole hedge is flat against the house. What could've done that? Those branches are as tough as steel."

Some of Diego's neighbors moved closer, peering at the peculiar damage. Diego kept staring at Magnifico, who at a height of a little more than a mile, finally looked around, spurting a tiny blast of flame from his nose.

"Tomorrow night," a low, rumbling voice called out in Diego's mind. "Prepare yourself, and bring the girl, Racquel, for in less than twenty-four hours you will see why your ancestors called upon you to guide mighty Magnifico on a journey of great importance."

"Mijo," said Diego's father.

Diego kept staring at the sky.

"Hey, hombre, you okay?" asked his father. "Let's go inside and have some hot chocolate."

Craning his neck, Diego stared into the heavens, watching Magnifico disappear into the stars.

CHAPTER TWENTY-TWO

"Just be waiting by your window tonight about midnight," said Diego to Racquel as they walked through the gates of their elementary school.

"Why? What's going to happen?"

"I can't tell you because I don't know everything. Magnifico said I have to bring you along on the next journey."

"He said he wanted me to go with you?" she asked, excitedly.

"Yes, but I wouldn't be too happy about it."

"Why not?" asked Racquel, still unwilling to tell Diego about her role in his journey. "Who wouldn't go crazy for an adventure like that?"

"Look Racquel, Magnifico isn't a toy dragon. He's not a statue either. He's bigger than a five-story building, he breathes fire, and sometimes he's pretty mean."

"Then why are you going with him? Aren't you afraid he might hurt you, or me, or get us both in trouble somehow?"

"It's not like that," said Diego. "He's just unpredictable, that's all, and if he wanted to he could wipe out an entire army."

Racquel looked at Diego as if he had lost his mind. "You don't really mean that, do you?"

Diego stared at her silently. The final bell rolled around the hallways.

"Well?"

"Did you read about the explosion last night?" he asked.

"That was him, Magnifico, I mean?"

"Yes, and he blew every circuit for a half mile around my neighborhood. All the power everywhere, gone, just like that."

"Why? You must have done something to upset him."

Again Diego gazed into Racquel's prying eyes.

"Well?" she asked.

"He sneezed."

"What?"

"That's right. My father caught us in the side yard. Magnifico had no time to change his shape or become invisible, so he hid in the trees against the wall. I guess the scent in the branches must have tickled his nose."

"One little sneeze did that?"

"Just imagine," said Diego, "what would happen if he really got angry."

"I don't even want to think about it," said Racquel.

"Then be ready at midnight outside of your house."

Later that day at lunch, Diego ran into Ricardo and Jose. He'd been thinking so hard about Magnifico that he almost walked right by them as they called out to him.

"Hey, estupido!" yelled Jose. "Don't you know who your friends are anymore?"

When Diego finally turned to see who had called him a dummy, he smiled broadly and ran over to his friends. With everything that had been happening, he hadn't seen his best buddies in days.

"Que pasa, hombres?" he said, slapping their hands playfully as they greeted each other.

"You in love or something?" asked Ricardo. "Ever since that crazy statue came into your life we haven't seen you at all."

"Si," said Jose, "but we've heard all kinds of things about you and Racquel."

"What kinds of things?" asked Diego, half offended and half thrilled.

"Nada," said Ricardo. "Just little stuff, like you and her meeting in the theater room from time to time."

"We only went there once. It was nothing."

"That's not what we heard, and now we know it's true," said Jose, falling into a playful prank. "Oh, Diego, love of my heart, kiss me again, please." Both boys laughed, pursing their lips together and making kissing noises as they crossed their arms.

Diego punched Jose's arm, hard. The two boys laughed even harder after seeing Diego's face light up like a stoplight. Ricardo embraced himself harder, making it look as though he was hugging a girl.

"Oh, Diego, kiss me again," he said.

Diego slammed his fist on Ricardo's right thigh. But when he saw how much fun his friends were having at his expense, he got caught in their hysterics. He wrestled both boys to the ground, laughing along with them. It was the first time in weeks he had really let loose, and it felt good.

"You're loco, both of you," he said after the three of them got up and began brushing off their jeans. "I'm glad I ran into you guys. It feels good to laugh."

The first bell sounded, ending the lunch period. Diego turned, looking in the direction of his next class.

"Un momento, amigo," said Ricardo, grabbing Diego's arm. "We want details."

"Si, Diego," said Jose. "What about you and Racquel? Are you two together, or what?"

"I think she just likes Magnifico," he told his friends. "She's just using me to be around him."

"A stupid statue?" asked Jose. "Are you serious?"

"I don't know *what's* going on, really."

"Then you're blind," said Ricardo. "We see the way she looks at you, and the way you act when you're around her."

Jose mimicked Diego melting away at the sight of Racquel. Diego laughed again as he walked away toward his next class.

"Tell me you wouldn't feel the same way," said Diego. "Look at it this way, I get to hang around with her and you two bozos get to hang around with each other. What would you rather do?"

Jose flung his pen at Diego, bouncing it harmlessly off his arm. "Eleven years old and already married."

"Oh, Racquel, love of my life," repeated the two boys as they ran off to class. "See you at lunch, joto!"

The second bell sounded across campus as Diego ran toward his class. He saw some of Racquel's friends and waved before ducking into his room.

Later, in the lunchroom, Diego, Jose, and Ricardo sat at a long table with Racquel and a few of her friends. They ate and talked, mostly about their plans for the weekend. Diego kept sneaking glances at Racquel. She had worn his favorite shirt to school, a purple, short-sleeved top. As he sat there in a daze, he heard a voice behind him mention his father.

"The stupid idiot probably left the gas on and went out to have a smoke," laughed one boy.

"The whole family's like that," said another. "His Dad's a dumb ass. His brother's a drunk, and who knows what his Mom is like."

Diego flew over the table before anyone else knew what was happening. He grabbed the hair of the boy with the big mouth and dragged him away from his seat. In his furious state, all he wanted to do was smash the boy's face into the ground.

The fight ended in seconds. Two security guards and a teacher separated Diego from his victim. Spitting like a madman, Diego told the boy if he ever heard him talk about his family like that again he'd regret it. The burly guards dragged the boys off in different directions.

Diego struggled against the strong arms of Hector. "¿Que pasa, Diego?" the big man asked. "What the heck happened back there?"

"Nada."

"Didn't look like nothing to me, mijo. You were going to kill that kid."

"He called my Dad a dumbass," said Diego.

"That's muy malo, for sure."

"He said worse about my mother. He doesn't even know my family at all. Why would he say stupid things like that?"

"I think you just answered your own question, kid," said Hector. "Some people, heck, *most* people are pretty damn stupid."

Diego struggled to get out of Hector's grip, but the guard held him easily. "No way, Diego, you have to go with me, and I have to make sure you don't run off and do something stupid."

"Let me go!"

"Nada, mijo. It's for your own good."

Diego thought about Magnifico for a second. Maybe tonight he could convince him to find that idiot's house and turn it into a pile of ashes. The voice of the vice-principal's secretary jarred him out of his daydream.

"Diego Ramirez, are you here again, and this time for starting a fight?"

"I didn't start it!" he yelled.

"That's not what I heard," said Mr. Baker. The imposing man stood in the doorway of his office. "Come into my office, Diego. I've called your parents. Your father is on his way to pick you up."

"What for?" he asked.

"Automatic three day suspension, son. You know the rules." Mr. Baker turned to Hector. "That will be all. Thank you for guiding Mr. Ramirez to my office."

Diego sat down hard on the old couch. Looking back briefly at Hector, he shook his head as he saw the large security guard give him a thumbs up.

"What's with you, mijo?" asked his father. "Your mother is at home crying. She thinks you're going to turn into another wanderer like Esteban.

"What do you think?" asked Diego.

"I don't know what to think. First, you get that dragon statue and then your life goes downhill. You've gotten into more trouble at school in the last month than in all the years leading up to the sixth grade, and now you're fighting? Is that how we brought you up?"

"I'm sorry, Papa, I don't know what happened. I heard that boy talking bad about you and Mama and I just snapped. All I wanted to do was rip his mouth out of his face so he wouldn't be able to say those things anymore."

"It's okay that you got mad, mijo," said his father. "It's even alright if you get into a scrape every now and then."

"Then what's the problem?"

"You started the fight, mijo. I don't ever want to hear about you getting tough like that again, you understand?"

Diego started to protest, but his father held up a calloused hand.

"If you can't avoid it and you have to fight, I understand, son. But don't ever throw the first punch. Bad things happen when you do that, and I love you too much to lose you over something as harmless as an insult."

"But he called you a dumbass, Papa."

"So what? Does that mean I'm a dumbass?"

"No, but who the hell is he to talk like that?"

"Watch yourself, mijo. In a minute, you'll be explaining yourself to your mother. If she hears words like that come out of your mouth she'll skin both of us alive."

"Then what am I supposed to do?" asked Diego.

"Tell him to shut his fat mouth," said his father. "Let him come after you, and if he hits you first, then you have my permission to put him down."

Diego smiled as he punched his father in the shoulder. His father was so strong it felt like his fist hit a fence post. Then he leapt at his father, hugging him fiercely.

"I love you, Papa, you're the best."

"I love you, too, mijo, don't ever forget that. What I do, I do for your own good."

"I know, Papa. Thanks."

"Don't thank me yet. We still have to face your Mama when we get home. If you think I'm angry, wait 'til you see her."

"We can handle her together," said Diego, hugging his father again.

"Not me, mijo, you're on your own."

CHAPTER TWENTY-THREE

"Diego!" said his mother sternly as soon as he and his father walked through the kitchen door. After she saw his face, her demeanor became more loving. "Are you all right?"

"Si, Mama," he said. "It was a stupid fight."

"Sit down, niñito. I wish to talk with you."

Diego looked at his father, who conveniently turned the other way.

"Don't look to him for support," she said, "he knows how upset I am about this."

"But, Mama,"

"Don't you but Mama me, señor. This is serious, and we're going to get to the bottom of it right now. Sit down, Diego. We have some questions for you."

Diego sat heavily on one the kitchen stools.

"We asked you a few days ago to find Mr. Sullivan's cell phone number. Do you have it for us?"

Diego froze. He'd forgotten all about it. With all the madness at school, it had slipped his mind completely. "No, Mama, and I don't think I'll be able to get it after all."

"Why not?" she asked.

"I guess he's pretty hard to get a hold of."

"Why? He came to the house easily enough when we invited him for dinner."

"Things have changed."

"What do you mean?" asked his mother. "What sort of things?"

Diego felt worn out. So much had happened in the last few weeks, he just didn't have any strength left. He decided the best course was to be honest with his parents.

"Well, for one," he said, "Magnifico isn't only a statue. He's actually a real dragon. He came to life at school a few weeks ago, and ever since then things have been getting loco."

Diego's mother and father stared at him as if he was a stranger. They looked to each other for explanations, and then back at Diego.

"It's true. Last night, when the power went out, it was because of Magnifico! He was hiding in the bushes on the side of the house when the flowers made him sneeze."

"Diego Ramirez!" interrupted his mother. "How dare you try to fill our heads with such nonsense. I'd say winning that dragon statue has made you muy loco."

"No, Mama, it's all true! He came alive in the library and tried to bite a couple of students! Then he tried to spit fire at Ricardo. Magnifico is *real*, Mama, the next time he appears I'll show you."

Diego's mother looked at her husband. Her eyes blazed with the same mysterious fire that convinced him to marry her over two decades ago, and as before, he knew her intent all too well.

"Diego," he said forcefully, "bring me the dragon statue, right now."

"I can't, Papa."

"You're in trouble, mijo. Stop this foolishness. Go into your room and bring Magnifico to me."

"He's not in my room anymore, Papa."

"Then where is he?" asked his father. "Where is the statue?"

"Gone," said Diego, "and I don't know where."

CHAPTER TWENTY-FOUR

"Is everything ready?"

"Yes," answered Magnifico. "Diego and the girl will be ready tonight at midnight."

"And Marisol?" asked Sullivan.

"She appeared last night in Diego's vision. I see no reason why she should not depart from the dream world and lead him toward his destiny."

"Let us hope so. Diego's people have waited too long for a guide to lead them along the path."

Sullivan looked across his living room at Magnifico. Barely six feet in height in his current form, the gleaming dragon sat against the far wall preening his powerful wings. He rarely made eye contact with Sullivan during their conversations, but at this moment, he caught the man's gaze.

"What if he fails?" asked Sullivan.

"He won't." said Magnifico.

"How can you be so certain? He's just a boy."

"He is the guide, even you agreed to that fact."

Magnifico released a long, rumbling growl. He had served people for over fifteen thousand years, and if he'd learned one thing, it was that humans were unpredictable. Even with as much confidence as he had in Diego, for all they knew he would panic at the worst possible time. All their dreams, their hopes, everything they'd planned for would disappear in an instant.

"What of the girl, Racquel?" he asked the author.

"She has her own role to play in this journey. If Diego gets nervous, she will steer him back toward the correct path. After that, her true purpose will be revealed to him."

"Hmmm," grumbled Magnifico, letting a stream of dark orange smoke drift up from his nostrils. "Perhaps you're right."

The dragon sat thoughtfully, going over a hundred possible scenarios in his mind.

CHAPTER TWENTY-FIVE

"You're grounded, mijo," said Diego's father. "You've upset your mother and disappointed me as well. You're staying in your room until we figure out how long to punish you."

"Papa, no!" screamed Diego, thinking about his promise to Magnifico. He thought fast. "What about my soccer games? My team needs me."

His father held up a thick, tanned palm. "I don't mind when you do something dumb as long as I'm the only one who knows, but when you make your mother cry that's the end of it." Diego's father walked toward the door, opened it, and looked back at the son he loved more than his own life. "I'll bring your dinner in about an hour, mijo. You stay in your room until then. Comprende?"

"Si, Papa, I will."

Diego heard the door slide past the swollen frame and finally shut. *He's really pissed at me this time,* he thought, *how am I going to sneak out tonight? He'll be listening for anything.*

The ring tone on his cell phone jolted him from his thoughts. He snatched the phone from his backpack and answered it as fast as he could. *If Mama heard this,* he thought, *she'd no doubt come in here and take my phone away.* He looked at the screen before answering.

"Racquel?" he said softly.

"Diego," she said, "why are you whispering?"

He realized how silly it was, with his parents so far away in the kitchen. "Racquel, where are you?"

"Home, silly, where else would I be?"

"My parents grounded me," said Diego.

"What? What about tonight?"

"I don't know. There's nothing I can do. My Dad's really mad this time."

"What if Magnifico gets upset? He might just decide to take a bath in your pool while he burns your house to the ground."

Diego pondered that for a moment. The dragon was impulsive, but he didn't think he'd go that far. "No, they want me to do something, so torching my house isn't an option."

"What do you mean, they want you to do something?"

"Magnifico and Mr. Sullivan keep talking about me being a guide, whatever that is, and how I've got the blood of Mexican heroes in my body. It's pretty weird, but kind of cool, too."

Racquel listened with delight. She was obedient to a fault, earned good grades, and she was polite to her family's friends, but she loved an adventure now and then.

"Well," she said, "we have to meet him tonight."

"Who?"

"Magnifico. We'd better be waiting for him at midnight like he said. I'd rather not find out what they're up to the hard way."

"Racquel, I can't," said Diego. "My Dad, he'll..."

"And what if you *do* have the blood of our heroes in your veins? Would they turn away from an adventure like this?"

"No, I guess not."

"Then we can't either, Diego. I don't care how you do it, but you have to be standing in your yard at midnight. I'll be waiting for you and Magnifico to come get me." She listened to a dead phone for a second. "Okay?"

"Yeah," said Diego. "Yeah, okay. I'll be out there tonight."

"Good."

An awkward silence followed her last comment. Racquel was dying to ask a certain question, but she wondered if Diego could answer it, or handle it at this point.

After a moment, she blurted it out. "Diego, where are we going, and what's going to happen when we get there?"

"I guess we'll find out tonight," said Diego, feeling his stomach rumble for the first time that evening.

Diego had barely snapped his phone shut when he heard soft knuckles tapping on his bedroom door. His father's smiling face peered through the crack. He carried a steaming bowl of albondigas soup and a container of tortillas. Diego inhaled the wonderful smell of his mother's cooking. He smiled as his father set the tray on his bed. He dipped a warm tortilla into the broth and took a healthy bite. When he looked up his mother was standing next to his father.

"How does it taste, carita?"

"Delicioso, Mama," said Diego. "You're the best cook in the whole world."

She smiled at her son. "We don't like punishing you, Diego, but we have to watch out for you. We're terrified that you'll end up like Esteban."

"I won't, Mama, you don't have to worry about that. Besides, Esteban isn't a bad brother. At least I don't think so. He went through a horrible time, that's all, and he's having trouble getting himself together. Don't you love Esteban anymore, Mama?"

"Of course I love him, Diego, but right now he's hurting himself, and he's hurting this family. We can't allow him to be around us until he's figured everything out."

Diego's mother reached over and caressed the back of his neck. She smiled as he pulled huge spoonfuls of soup up to his mouth, hungrily slurping up tender meatballs and vegetables. With the bowl drained except for a drizzle of broth, Diego wiped his mouth with a tortilla and gulped it down. He held the bowl up to his mother, smiling his cutest *I'm your favorite son* smile for her.

"More?" she asked, pleased to see her son eating heartily. She took the bowl from Diego, smacked her husband on the shoulder and turned toward the door. "You keep eating like that and you're going to end up looking like your father, El Gordo."

Diego and Alvaro laughed as Alejandra walked down the hall toward the kitchen.

At eleven-fifty that night, the alarm on Diego's cell phone beeped quietly. He had set it before going to bed, stuffing it under his pillow so no one would hear it. Breathing evenly and quietly, he listened for any sounds coming from down the hall. He heard his father's muffled snoring, loud and long even with two doors closed between the rooms.

When he felt certain his parents were asleep, he silently slid out from under the covers. Already clad in jeans and tennis shoes, he threw a t-shirt and sweatshirt over his shoulders. Before tip-toeing to the sliding glass door, he pulled a dark baseball cap over his head.

As quietly as he could, he lifted the lock on the door. The door opened without making a sound. He looked out toward the pool, and then stepped through the doorway.

"Mijo?" asked Alvaro gruffly, "where are you going?"

CHAPTER TWENTY-SIX

Diego froze. He didn't know what to do or say. He couldn't look any guiltier if he had said goodbye to his parents before leaving.

"Papa, I was just going to... I mean..."

"Come back inside, mijo. Close the door behind you."

Diego couldn't do anything but obey. He'd been caught and now he had to face his father. He stepped back into his room and slid the door shut.

"What are you up to, Diego?" asked his father. When he saw his son sitting silently, he used a tone of voice he rarely displayed. "Mijo! *Tell me now!*"

"Papa," he blurted, a single tear moistening his eye. "I told you! It's Magnifico! He's waiting outside for me right now. He's taking me somewhere tonight."

"The statue?" asked his father. "It's outside right now, waiting for you?"

"Not the statue, Papa, Magnifico! He's a real dragon!"

His father took him by the arm and led him to the sliding glass door. Throwing the handle back gruffly, he escorted his son out to the pool.

"Where is he, this dragon of yours?"

"Out there, through the gate, in the side yard."

The gate latch flew open. Seconds later Diego and his father stood in the yard.

"Where?" demanded his father.

Diego quickly scoped out the yard. Seeing no sign of Magnifico, he looked at the only place he'd knew he'd find him.

"Up there, Papa," he said, "on the roof."

Diego's father angrily twisted his aching neck as he looked up to the slate shake roof he had installed less than a year ago. What looked down upon him made him stagger backwards.

Magnifico sat perched atop the Ramirez home in all of his dazzling glory. Almost fifty feet tall, with a wingspan twice his height, he flashed his blazing eyes at Diego and his frightened father. Smoke and flame licked the spaces where his teeth didn't quite fit together within his massive jaws.

His huge, calloused feet nearly covered the width of the house. The giant talons crumpled the shake roof, letting the crumbs dribble into the yard below.

With a grunt and a blast of smoke, Magnifico jumped from the rooftop to the yard. Flapping his mighty wings, he landed softly next to Diego's father.

"Will you not introduce us?" he asked Diego.

"Papa," said Diego, looking at the awestruck man next to him. "This is Magnifico, the dragon statue I won at school."

Alvaro's jaws hung open. His lungs sagged, inhaling no air. Diego's father stood like a man who had seen his own death.

"Magnifico, this is my father."

"Mucho gusto, señor," said the dragon, smiling slyly.

Alvaro tried his best to say something, anything, but his jaws wouldn't move. He eyes, wide as baseballs and trembling with fear, looked up and down and side to side. He could see no end to the giant monster standing in his yard. His only sign of life occurred when he moved in front of his son in a protective stance.

"M-Magnifico?" he asked finally, shaking with dread.

"In the flesh. May I say that you have a very brave son, Señor, very brave indeed."

"W-What do you want with him? He's just a boy. Please, leave him alone. His mother is very worried."

"He is more than a boy, but not quite a man," said Magnifico. "That will be remedied tonight, though, I assure you."

Diego's father finally found his voice. "No! There will be no more adventures! If you are real, then fly away to wherever it is you call home. If you are only a dream, then disappear and let us sleep."

"You may go back into your home, now, Señor."

"What? ¿Estas estupido?" asked his father. "Vamos, before I call the police!"

"You may go back into your home, now, Señor," repeated Magnifico. "Go back to your wife. Tell her that Diego is safe in his bed. I wish a soothing night's rest for both of you."

Diego's father faltered for a moment. He seemed to want to argue further, but then, without a backwards glance, he turned and walked back through the gate.

Diego tensed; he couldn't understand why his father had walked away so meekly. He stood quietly until he heard the lock to his room latch into place. "What was that all about?" he asked excitedly. "What did you do to him?"

"Hurry, Guide, we have little time."

"No, wait!" asked Diego. What did you do to him? Have you hurt him?"

Magnifico lowered his wing toward Diego. He scraped the tip against the damp blades of grass on the lawn. "Your father is unharmed. I merely convinced him that after he came out to investigate he saw nothing but an empty yard. Right now he is crawling back into bed, assuring your mother that you are quite safe."

Diego scrambled up onto Magnifico, grasping the spikes as he pulled himself past the leathery scales. Even before he had reached the huge neck, Magnifico began slowly waving his monstrous wings. Diego sat in his familiar seat. He felt the dragon's muscles tense as he prepared for flight.

With two powerful thrusts, Magnifico pulled his bulk into the air over Diego's neighborhood. Had anyone been on a late night walk they might have missed Diego's dragon completely.

Two things happened immediately after they left the ground. First, the coloring on Magnifico's body assumed a shade identical to the dark night sky, rendering him invisible. Second, the roof of Diego's house quietly reassembled itself. To any of their neighbors, there wouldn't be anything outwardly different about their home. It looked as it always had, except for two immense claw prints impressed into the slate tiles.

Unlike the other flights, when Magnifico seemed not to care about anything other than floating on a warm updraft, on this night the dragon glared down at the city below. To Diego, it almost appeared as though Magnifico expected something to jump up from the streets and attack them.

After a few minutes, the dragon dipped his right wing low toward the ground. Diego felt the winds pushing against his body as he clung to the spike with both arms. He smiled, enjoying this flight much more than the previous trips. His legs and backside seemed to fit more easily against Magnifico's huge body. If they hadn't been turning so sharply, he might have removed his hands to see if he could stay aloft without holding on.

Magnifico leveled off before dipping his left wing. With the wind whipping through Diego's hair, he peered over his left side and spotted Racquel's house. She stood in the front yard awaiting their arrival. When she finally saw the giant dragon sailing over her home, her eyes opened wide with awe.

She smiled as the wind from Magnifico's wings rushed by her. The gust ruffled her jacket and hair, forcing her to step back a pace. Her excitement grew every second as she watched Diego gliding along on the dragon's shoulders.

Before she could wave to her boyfriend, Magnifico landed in her driveway. The spikes on the edge of the ribbed wings sliced through some fern trees along the lawn fronting Racquel's home, sending green, pungent sprays of grated leaves everywhere. Diego climbed down as soon as Magnifico's tail stretched out to allow Racquel passage onto the dragon's shoulders.

"C'mon," said Diego. "I'll help you up."

Racquel couldn't move. She looked at Magnifico's massive body and giggled with delight. She had always imagined a fantasy world filled with wonder, and here she stood gazing into the eyes of a creature out of her wildest imagination.

"Be quick, Guide," rumbled Magnifico. "We must leave at once if we are to find the window."

Diego grabbed Racquel's hand, pulling her aboard. "Racquel, meet Magnifico," he said, giving a hurried introduction. "Magnifico, this is Racquel. Be nice to her."

"Mucho gusto, Magnifico."

"El gusto es mio, señorita."

CHAPTER TWENTY-SEVEN

Marisol floated over the silent city, a spirit from the world of the dead. Lazily she drifted along the lonely downtown streets, seeking the only man who could give her comfort during her endless search for peace. Looking over and through buildings by the dozen, she finally saw him lounging alone in a public park at the center of town. He sat with his knees high and his elbows resting on the caps. His head hung low. Perhaps he was asleep or drunk again. She couldn't tell from a distance.

Marisol fell from the sky in waves. She would rise on a warm draft. Then after resting a bit, she would continue downward toward the park. Finally reaching a comfortable altitude, she circled the grounds a few times before landing lightly in front of Esteban.

Diego's brother sat against a gnarled oak tree. The base boasted the carvings of many a star-crossed couple, including Esteban and Marisol's initials encased inside a carefully sculpted heart. It was on this spot that Esteban rested the crown of his head.

With tears dotting his cheeks, he looked up at the beaming harvest moon. He remembered how much Marisol enjoyed the giant singing moon in the sky. When they sat out by the pool of his father's home, Marisol would sing sweet songs to Esteban, dangling his heart by a thread with every note. She was a beauty in so many ways; to lose her in the way he did had destroyed him. He could no more rise from the ashes of his sorrow than come back from the dead himself.

Marisol approached her boyfriend, the young man she had decided to spend the rest of her life with. She reached out, hoping to dry his cheeks and comfort his soul. As before, her transparent hand fell right through his skin. The half-dried tears remained, subtle markers of the depth of their love.

"Esteban," she cooed in a voice no one could hear but her. "You must go forward. You must move on with your life. It will break my heart to watch you waste away like this."

As if hearing her words, Esteban lifted his head. He sniffed the air, sensing an aroma that just that second had entered the park. He waved his hand back and forth in front of his face, feeling nothing. Then he lurched forward, right through the ghostly image of his girlfriend. Waving his arms about wildly, he screamed her name over and over, willing her to come back to him. Then he fell back against the tree, sobbing.

"Corazón," whispered Marisol. "No more of this. You must accept what has happened and find yourself again."

Just then, the faint roar of an ancient dragon fell from the sky above them. Marisol looked up, seeing the giant form of Magnifico soaring through the night sky. At such an altitude, he seemed to be nothing more than a small, shadowy cloud, but she knew differently. Magnifico had come to collect her, no doubt with Esteban's brother in tow.

She had always suspected something about Diego. Since first meeting him, she had seen a glint in his eyes, something passionate in his actions, and even a type of tranquil confidence in his voice. As she listened to the great dragon call to her again, she wondered exactly what she'd find when she saw Diego riding on its shoulder.

She cupped her hand under Esteban's chin one last time. "Sleep, my love, for tomorrow you will awaken to a better world."

CHAPTER TWENTY-EIGHT

Magnifico flew far above the park, surveying every square foot before descending. At such an early hour, he expected to see no one, and to his good fortune his suspicion had been correct. He saw only Diego's brother sitting numbly against a tree trunk.

"Do not call out to him," he said to Diego. "Leave him to his drunken thoughts. It is better for him to remain asleep as we pass over the city."

"Why are we here?" Diego asked. "If we're not going to do anything to save Esteban, them why show him to me?"

Magnifico snarled. "Don't worry about that one, Guide. He will figure into our journey soon enough."

Diego prepared to ask another question, but he felt a delicate finger tapping on his right shoulder. He turned and saw Racquel's eyes wide with fear and awe, for behind her sat a ghostly apparition of Marisol. The three small figures sat upon Magnifico's broad shoulders, looking at each other as if they'd met in a dream world.

Marisol smiled at Diego and Racquel. In her own wonderful way, she soothed their fears, even making them feel comfortable around her. She couldn't speak yet, but her eyes told the two young travelers to settle into their journey without fearing her.

"Diego," said Racquel, over the wailing wind whistling in their ears. "What in the name of God are we doing here?"

"I think I know. Somehow I think Marisol is here because of my brother, but we're here for a different reason."

Racquel smiled, once again reminded of Diego's intelligence. She hated keeping secrets from him, but she knew the truth of his journey would be revealed soon.

Diego turned again to face his girlfriend. "We'll all find out soon I'm sure." As he said this, he looked over her shoulder at Marisol, who smiled again. She motioned for them to hold on tightly. Diego wasted no time. He grabbed the spike and told Racquel to wrap her arms around his waist. Marisol seemed to float along on Magnifico's back without effort. The three of them felt the dragon's muscles tense as he thrust his wings ever harder.

In a matter of seconds their speed increased tenfold. Magnifico swirled, looped, and zoomed through the sky at incredible speed. Diego and Racquel gritted their teeth as they held on, gripping the sticky scales with their knees and feet. As his wings pumped even harder, they felt the muscles in Magnifico's shoulders straining underneath them. The giant dragon reached deep within his soul to find reserves he hadn't used in centuries. As he soared through the sky at a frightening speed, he inhaled giant plumes of oxygen into his belly and lungs. Huge volumes of air flew into his combustible insides, creating a supernatural fire.

When his lungs felt ready to burst, Magnifico released a flood of fire into the sky. His breath exploded in a rampaging discharge straight out from his spiked mouth. The flames gushed forward, hitting the wall of wind pushing against them. They peeled back into a tulip shaped curl of bluish fire.

The tips of the blowback twisted toward Diego and Racquel. Feeling the flames heating up their skin, they fought the urge to move back toward Magnifico's tail. Racquel did inch back a little until she felt Marisol's soft touch. She jumped. When she turned and saw Marisol's face, it comforted her enough to help her keep her seat.

Diego hadn't fared so well. Hoping to look brave for his girl-friend and his brother's girlfriend, he held on to the spike, defying the flames. His face grew warmer by the second, and he could smell his hair burning. Even his eyebrows became slightly singed; he wanted desperately to wipe away the scorched skin around them.

And still Magnifico's flame spewed forth. The torrents increased in volume and speed, until the back draft filled the sky in front of him. The fire's coloring began fluctuating wildly, changing hues a dozen times a second. Every possible color within the prism of life flashed before the giant dragon and his passengers. With each change the intensity grew and grew, until Diego and Racquel screamed within the fiery shower that had engulfed them. Magnifico added his powerful voice to the group, spitting the last of the flames from his insides.

In a spasm of space and sound, the fire vanished. The last of the flames disappeared behind Magnifico, drawn away by the powerful winds. All sound in the sky followed, leaving Diego, Racquel, and Marisol resting on Magnifico's back as he floated over an endless desert.

The scenery looked familiar to Diego. As Magnifico cruised lower he recognized it. It was the same desert they had visited the night before in his dream, the place where the misshapen ghosts wandered without purpose. The scene became clearer. Everything fell into place as Magnifico coasted a little more than a hundred yards above the rock strewn floor.

On and on they went, mile after mile, over the endless sands.

Diego and Racquel said nothing. They couldn't believe the beauty that lay before them. Nothing could compare with the desert under a starlit sky.

Finally, Magnifico executed a broad turn, coming about one hundred eighty degrees. It appeared to Diego that they would travel the sky above the desert again and again, seeing nor doing nothing of significance. He almost questioned the big dragon, when he suddenly felt the scaly belly swelling again. Magnifico was preparing for another inferno. Diego began to understand, and he reached around to grab Racquel's hands.

When he felt nothing behind him, he turned. Racquel and Marisol had disappeared. Diego opened his mouth to question Magnifico when the dragon's shoulders bucked violently. Nearly falling off his perch, he grabbed the spike and looked forward. The brilliant flames streamed forth from Magnifico's mouth, but this time the plumes descended toward the desert floor. Diego leaned over as far as he could. He watched the flames showering the sand and rocks with white-hot gushers. He felt so awed by what he saw next he forgot all about Racquel and Marisol.

The strange creatures from his dream returned, rising up out of the sand in great numbers. At first they looked like silt laden zombies, trudging along on a journey to nowhere. As the sand and debris fell away, however, Diego recognized them for what they were, the thousands of his countrymen and women who had died attempting the treacherous journey from their native land to America. They braved the passage for a land that promised opportunity perhaps not for them, but for their children and grandchildren. They had sacrificed their lives for a dream, a wish that they might escape poverty.

Collapsing in their own footsteps and falling to the desert floor, some had given way to delirium, actually packing more clothing on their backs under the blazing, punishing sun. Some had died with their dreams on their lips, gasping to the Holy Spirit for deliverance. Others had merely dropped to their knees, thinking they had found their new land, their salvation, and their futures. Their eyes had not deceived them, but their minds had given way to imagery caused by irrational hope.

As Magnifico cruised over the desert, blasting his magic fire, Diego sat fascinated by the scene unfolding before him. Thousands of people, old, young, and middle aged, rose up from the cool sand drifts after the enchanted fire passed over them. Their bodies reformed as they struggled to gain their feet. Diego craned his neck, looking behind him at the trail of fire left by Magnifico. A sea of people staggered after them, unsure of where to go. Some had been dead for so long they didn't even recognize their surroundings. He yelled at those who emerged from the sand, telling the people to follow Magnifico.

Before turning back around, Diego peered into the crowd, trying to locate Racquel and Marisol. There were too many people, however, and in a few moments he faced forward again.

Magnifico felt a series of pinpricks dotting his right leg. Craning his great neck slightly so as not to disturb the direction of the fire, he spied a small group of men standing guard on the Northern border. They fired their weapons without restraint, shooting at Diego, the people rising from the desert, and even at him. *The impudence,* he thought. He allowed a single stream of bristling fire to boil up in his nose. When he could no longer contain it, he clamped down on his left nostril and gave the right a mighty push.

A ball of fire two feet in diameter exploded from the opening.

Expanding after its release, the flaming sphere accelerated toward the men. Suddenly the roaring fireball split into a dozen smaller weapons. Every one of them sought out a different target.

The men on the ground refused to believe their eyes. They kept firing their weapons, and one managed to hit one of the speeding spheres. It exploded into a shower of crimson sparks. Every one of them came alive, sizzling madly as they sped toward them.

The men dropped guns, ammunition, and binoculars all at once and ran for their trucks. They had no chance to outrun Magnifico's magic, and soon the crackling fireballs slammed into the ground around their camp. The men jumped, dodged, and tried swatting the glowing spheres. They could do nothing to keep them away. The fireballs exploded everywhere, turning night into day.

Diego looked over Magnifico's right wing and smiled. He was glad the men weren't seriously harmed, but at the same time it was hilarious watching them try to outrun the streaking fireballs. He watched them run away from the border, happy that they wouldn't be taking potshots at his folk any longer.

My people, he thought. *There are so many.* Magnifico's magic fire had freed thousands from their soulless death in the border region of the desert. They milled about, greeting each other numbly, asking for help finding their families, their way home, or perhaps a bite to eat.

Diego had been so entranced by their appearance he hadn't noticed the silence surrounding him. Magnifico's breath had given out. The fire had extinguished itself, and they flew back and forth lazily among the meandering crowds.

Absentmindedly, Diego reached around behind his back. He expected to feel Racquel's hand grasping his, but then he remembered her disappearance. Frightened that she might have fallen off during the excitement, he leaned forward along the dragon's neck. "Magnifico," he called out to the rigid, spiked ear in front of him. "Where is Marisol? Has she taken Racquel away somewhere?"

The leathery skin rumbled beneath Diego's body. "There is always a price to pay," he said. "Even with the power of a guide, there must be a sacrifice."

Diego hammered his fist down onto Magnifico's ear. "What do you mean a sacrifice? Why didn't you say anything? I never would have let her come along if you had told us."

"She came with us of her own accord, Guide. Had you asked her, the outcome would have been the same. She would have agreed to come, and now she would be walking with Marisol in the land of the dead."

"No!"

"Never mind," thundered Magnifico. "The time has come. Your people cannot find their way home. Without you they will wither away as before, and this time there will be no return. Unless you show them the way back to their ancestral lands, their families will never have the chance to see them again. There will be no laughter, no sharing of food and drink, no music, no reunion at all. It is up to you, Guide."

"Tell me what to do!"

Magnifico's body bucked violently. Diego feared he might have angered the giant dragon. He half expected to find himself tumbling through thin air any second.

"Think, boy," said Magnifico. "Do you remember what Nathan and I told you? You share the blood of the greatest heroes your people have ever known. Can you not find it within you to lead all those you see below you to safety?"

Diego wanted to order Magnifico to land and set him free

so he could find his girlfriend. He wanted to pinch himself and wake from what he hoped would be another in a series of strange dreams.

He glanced down at the people stumbling about in the desert. He saw men, women, young and old, and even children hanging onto their parent's hands. A pang of guilt swept over him. He had acted selfishly. *Magnifico is right. The people needed my guidance.* He asked Christ to protect Racquel until he could find her again.

"Alright, *dragon*," he said in a commanding voice. "Fly west, as far as possible, until we find the beginning of the line. Let loose a loud roar when we reach that point."

Magnifico turned sharply. When he felt the boy's legs and feet clutching his neck firmly, a smile spread from one ear to the other. He pumped his great wings with all his strength, hoping to cut the trip short. On a whim, he unleashed a wicked snarl as he lifted his guide into the sky.

CHAPTER TWENTY-NINE

The wind whipped through Diego's hair, whistling past his ears with an ever-increasing pitch. He held on, excited but scared as Magnifico raced toward the west end of the crowd. Straining to see through the slits of his tear-streaked eyes, he tried to focus on their destination. It didn't help that a blazing summer sun lay low in the sky directly ahead of them. Diego cradled the spike as tightly as he could, scrunching his legs against Magnifico's neck. He closed his eyes as the dragon went supersonic.

Magnifico finally dipped his left wing, executing a high-speed turn over the far end of the staggering crowd. He bellowed a deep greeting to all below him, causing hundreds of Diego's people to peer into the sky in wonder. He circled, slowly decreasing his speed so his guide would have time to readjust.

Diego cracked his eyes open. He quickly shut them again after seeing a ball of fire consuming the sky ahead of him. At length he peeked again, and this time he kept his eyes open. His jaw dropped, he tried to speak but couldn't, for the burning globe captured his mind completely. He released his hold on the spike, leveling his hands in front of his face.

The sun had grown to monstrous proportions. It covered the horizon, the intense shoots of fire blasting in every direction. Something moved within the fire, something more than just flickering bullets of flame. Animals danced, crying in happiness or seeking deliverance, Diego could not tell which.

Magnifico's body bristled. He called out to the creatures swirling within the flames, imploring them to join him for a frolicking flight around the earth. Some of the dashing shapes answered back, but none came forth to join him. This seemed to agitate Magnifico to no end, and he bellowed anew as he saw more of his brothers and sisters appear. He lurched forward toward the sun, almost forgetting his duty to Diego. He was a child yearning to return home to his mother, a lost dragon pup calling out to the skies to show him the way home. He circled, edging closer to the sun, and then executed the same maneuver numerous times. He nearly dumped his guide in the desert and soared home to his birthplace.

"Now, Magnifico," said Diego. "To the people!"

Logic replaced insanity, and he yanked his anxious spirit back into his soul. Arcing back toward the desert floor, he looked up at Diego with an expression of shame, if a dragon could host such an emotion.

What he saw sitting astride his back caused the feeling to fall away like an old scale. Diego sat tall and proud, a new bearing apparent in his posture. His eyes burned like the sun he had seen only a moment before. His hand and arm, ablaze with fire that could only have come from the heavens, served as a beacon to his people. He held his fist high above his head, where those on the ground could see it for miles in every direction.

Diego had finally assumed his role as guide to the thousands of people below him. Magnifico watched the boy as he peered down over his wing, swirling his arm back and forth so the crowd could find their way.

One by one and then by the dozen, and finally in larger groups,

Diego's people looked up. If they saw Magnifico underneath Diego's body, they gave no indication, for their eyes stayed with the living torch their guide held high above them. Magnifico soared down toward the crowd, leveling off at just over fifty feet. As he glided over them, Diego passed more energy to his torch.

The people raised their arms in greeting. Their bodies floated into the sky, lifted off the ground by a force Diego commanded. They followed along in Magnifico's wake, buoyed by the magic of the Sol Dragones.

They smiled and laughed, seemingly content with their sudden abilities. Several even danced together in the sky, holding hands and celebrating the return of the guide they had waited so long to meet.

Diego called down, urging more to follow him. He shouted encouragement in the language of his ancestors, willing the people to have courage. Magnifico bellowed mightily. His roar cascaded along the desert floor, carrying more of Diego's people aloft. As the dragon soared, the floating parade of people trailed behind his massive, spiked tail like a Revolution Day parade.

Soon Diego and Magnifico had collected every lost soul from the desolate wilderness. The spirits of thousands glided along, flapping lazily in the breeze.

Magnifico lowered his tail and raised his chin up to the sky. Up and farther up he flew, heading straight toward the blazing sun. He roared again, a signal to his kind that he was returning with a gift for the Gods.

Diego stretched his fist outward, straight toward the origin of his newfound power. The eternal light shining forth from his arm rolled away from his shoulder, popping off his fist like a sparkler. After watching the flame extinguish itself, he turned once, checking on the mile-long swath of spirits following behind them. He saw his people smiling, beaming with the thought of finally reaching a place of peace.

Turning forward again, he saw nothing but the immense surface of the sun. He heard Magnifico calling out to the fire, roaring repeatedly, and as they flew closer, Diego heard faint sounds coming from within the inferno. He could barely hear them, but he knew they had to be other dragons. They sounded exactly like those he heard when taking pictures with Mr. Sullivan in the library. It might be Magnifico's family, or his kind, or both. He felt certain about one thing, though; there were hundreds of them.

Magnifico turned, dashing across the face of the sun. Roaring one last time, he flew closer to the thunderous columns of fire. Diego felt no warmth on his face or hands. Instead of heat, he sensed a huge surge of incredible power.

Then the dragons appeared. Emerging from the flames one by one, they roared their greetings to Magnifico. On they came, pumping their wings as they flew toward their brother. To Diego, it looked like a squadron of warriors heading into battle. No two dragons looked identical. None of them looked perfectly black like Magnifico. No matter what their coloring, though, each of them looked fierce and capable.

Dozens of gigantic dragons swirled all about Magnifico. Diego sat in a daze watching them soar in every direction. Some flew close by their brother for a moment before veering off again, nearly whisking Diego off his perch. None of them took notice of the lengthy trail of spirits as they soared through the sky. It seemed they understood why the people trailed behind Magnifico.

Suddenly, Diego's dragon released a deafening roar. The accompanying dragons fell into line beside and behind him, flying steadily along his wings and tail. Another earsplitting roar echoed around the sky, and then Magnifico turned to look back at the people Diego had guided from the desert graveyard to the heavens.

He flicked his tail once, shaking off fifty of the traveling spirits. One of the companion dragons dropped out of formation, scooping them up in her wake. She flew gently, allowing her passengers to attach themselves to her tail. In a few moments, they trailed behind her as they had behind Magnifico. With a parting roar, she departed from the group and flew straight toward the sun.

With the first group sent toward their final resting place, Magnifico again snapped his tail. Groups of fifty travelers flew in every direction, separated from the main flock. Diego covered his ears as the remaining dragons hailed their brother as they gathered their charges.

Diego watched the people vanish into the sun. One by one, the dragons disappeared, taking the spirits along with them. He couldn't think of anything to say. He sat in awe of what he had just witnessed.

"Do you understand your purpose, now?" asked Magnifico, interrupting his thoughts.

"I know why you and Mr. Sullivan summoned me," said Diego.

"Then tell me, Guide."

"My people would never have been able to rest in the cold loneliness of the desert. Their spirits would always wander aimlessly had we not come along and shown them the way."

"The way to where, Diego?"

"Home."

"It is enough that you comprehend the sun's significance as

the home of your families and friends. Now that we have accomplished what we set out to do, we must arrange for payment."

Diego snapped out of his transfixed state. "Payment? What do you mean, dragon?"

Magnifico soared away from the sun, riding the jet stream back toward Diego's home. "There must always be an exchange, Diego, whenever the Gods grant one's wishes."

"What do you mean?" asked Diego. "Stop, stop flying right now! Answer my question. What do you mean by an exchange?"

"The price for the freedom of those trapped in the desert, Guide. It was her wish, after all."

Diego opened his mouth to protest, but his thoughts stopped him. He turned, holding the huge shoulder spike in his left hand. A ghostly image of Racquel sat behind him.

"No!" he yelled. "Bring her back!"

Magnifico did not reply. Flapping his wings evenly, he peered down toward the city lights. They had passed beyond the desert border quickly, almost as if by magic. Soon the city turned to suburbs, and when he spotted Diego's home, he soared over the rebuilt roof and on toward the horse trail surrounding the neighborhood. When he felt certain no one occupied the riding ring the trail surrounded, he set down, barely disturbing the groomed surface of the soil.

Diego jumped from his seat. With fire in his eyes, he ran around to face Magnifico. He grabbed one of the larger spikes on the dragon's lower jaw and pulled himself closer.

"Where is she?" he demanded.

"With Marisol, Diego," said Magnifico. "It was her wish from the beginning."

"No! I don't believe it."

"It's true, Diego," said a voice calling out from behind him. "She made her choice long ago."

Diego turned to see Sullivan walking up behind him. He looked refreshed, as if he'd taken a long shower and dressed for the occasion. He wore a tranquil smile on his face.

Diego stared hard at him. "What do you mean, she made her choice? If either one of us had known what you and your dragon friend were up to, we'd never have gone along on this loco journey."

"¿Loco?" roared Magnifico as he turned his massive head in Diego's direction. "Who are *you* to insult the creator, the protector of the people since long before you were born?"

Diego tried to cut in, but Magnifico brought his forepaw down onto the riding ring with such force it knocked both Sullivan and him to the ground.

"Be silent!" commanded the dragon, hot ash billowing from his trembling jaws. "Would you have us reverse all the good we've done this night? Would that be your decision, oh wise Guide?" His scaled face pinched in disgust. His spiked tail swept around, forcing Diego onto his feet. "I will no longer act as transport to this selfish creature, Nathan. He is not worthy to wear the name guide."

"You will do as the Sol Dragones instruct!" countered Sullivan. "Face us, now!"

Magnifico's blood boiled. *If I had only turned away all those centuries ago,* he thought. *I should have known better than to swear my allegiance to such selfish creatures.* He twisted his neck, lunging around and toward Sullivan. Snapping his jaws an inch away from the man's nose, he reared back, rumbling and snarling as he did. Blood red plumes of fire shot skyward from his nostrils.

"Are you finished?" asked Sullivan. He looked around to find Diego. The boy had scampered to the other side of the rink. With eyes wide, he clung to the rickety railing with all his might. "Now that you've undone all the goodwill we worked so hard to instill into our guide, perhaps you'd care to share your next move with me."

Sullivan turned, calmly walking over to Diego. Squatting down, he looked him in the eye and smiled. "Don't let him fool you. Although he could destroy almost anything, to you and me he's quite harmless."

Diego grasped the railing tightly. He kept his feet turned to the side, though, in case Magnifico got angry again. Wings or not, if another outburst erupted, the dragon would never find him again.

"Come, Diego," said Sullivan. "He wants to apologize."

Diego's eyes never left the dragon. He heard Sullivan's assurances, but the sight of the jaws clamping down in front of the man would not leave his mind.

"Okay," he said, "but you first."

"Good boy, now come on."

Magnifico's mood had cooled somewhat by the time Diego reached the center of the ring. His foot stomping, fire snorting, and snarling had disappeared. In their place lay the twisted expression of someone trying to be nice while still quite angry. "I am sorry, Diego, for my outburst, and I understand your anger regarding Racquel. Perhaps Nathan can explain what was in her heart better than I."

"You see, Diego?" asked Sullivan. "All is well again." He shot Magnifico a threatening look, in case the dragon felt the need to act stupidly again.

"What about Racquel?" asked Diego. "What did Magnifico mean by a sacrifice?"

"Balance is vital to the universe, Diego. Without it, none of our worlds would exist. When something is removed, something else must replace it."

"That's great," said Diego, "but when are you going to tell me about Racquel?"

Sullivan smiled, a grin saved for teachers taken to task by a student. "Many of Racquel's extended family lay in the very desert you and Magnifico visited tonight. Do you understand, Diego?"

The boy nodded.

"When we presented the idea to Racquel she agreed immediately. She gladly stepped into the passageway behind Marisol. With this selfless act she not only freed her family members, but all the people trapped within the mysterious sands. She is wise beyond her years, young man, the same as you."

The barest hint of a smile crept onto Diego's face. He felt heartbroken, though, at the thought of losing Racquel. He imagined her parents' suffering when they discovered she had left them, even for a cause as noble as this one.

"When will she come back to us, come home, I mean?"

Sullivan looked at Magnifico. The huge dragon shifted his body slightly, turning to face his guide. "That, Diego, is entirely up to you."

This time Diego lost his temper.

"Why?" he demanded. "I did everything you asked, and now her life depends on me? Why is it up to me?"

Sullivan moved to answer Diego, but Magnifico hushed him with a terse exhale. "You have not allowed me to finish, Guide. As a gift for your heroic journey, you will choose who will be able to return from the land of the dead. Once you make your selection it can never be reversed, so think hard, Diego."

"I pick Racquel," he said quickly.

"Don't you want to know who else waits beyond the barrier?"

He didn't care. All he wanted to do was get Racquel and go home. "Alright, who else is there?"

Magnifico inhaled deeply. With the softness of a spring breeze, he blew a shimmering cloud of smoke into the riding ring. It looked as though it might simply drift away, but instead it gathered itself into a tight cloud. It moved toward Diego and the author, settling in front of them. The mists changed, becoming less dense and more like a screen.

Racquel and Marisol stepped out of the swirling haze, with another young woman Diego didn't know. Still in spirit form, they greeted Magnifico and his friends. Smiling at Diego, Racquel greeted him warmly.

"You've done it, Diego. You freed our people from their endless sleep in the desert."

"And your family?" he asked. "Are they safe?"

"Yes. They have finally returned home. My grandfather's father thanks you for your courage."

"Your choice, Diego?" asked Magnifico.

Marisol stepped in front of Racquel. Since she couldn't grasp Diego's hand, she pursed her lips and used the wind of the spirits to blow the hair away from his forehead. "It is good to see you, hermanito. I'm proud of you, Diego, as are all the people."

Diego stuttered. "M-Marisol, I don't understand. What's going on here?"

"Make your choice, Diego," said Sullivan.

"Just wait!" he shouted. "I'll make it when I'm *ready!*"

Sullivan shot a glance at Magnifico. He saw the dragon's lips curl into a barely hidden smirk. "Alright, Diego, but remember, time is of the essence."

"Marisol," said Diego, "who is the other woman with you? Why has she come with you and Racquel?"

Marisol stepped aside and gave the strange woman the space she needed to come forward. The stranger kept her eyes lowered until she stood next to Marisol and Racquel. Then she lifted her chin and looked at Diego.

She seemed younger than Marisol, but only by some months or maybe a year. She looked plain but pretty, and smart, Diego could see this. She smiled at him.

"What is your name?" he asked.

"Catalina," she answered, quietly.

"Why are you here?"

"To help you make your choice."

"I don't want to make this choice!" he shouted as he stamped his foot.

Racquel broke Diego's mood. Stepping up to him, she lowered her head and looked into his eyes. When she made contact, she lifted her chin so Diego could follow. Soon, the pained expression on Diego's face melted away.

"I want you to come home," he said.

"This isn't about me, Diego, or you. It's not about what either of us wants. I had to do this, don't you see?"

She smiled, and in that grin Diego discovered the truth. He looked at Marisol, and then at the strange young woman. Catalina smiled at Diego, knowing what he would say before he thought of it.

"Pick from your heart, Diego," she said, softly. You're sure to be content if you follow that path."

"It is time, Guide," said Magnifico. "Make your selection."

Once again, Diego understood the meaning of his title. Thinking of Esteban, he extended a hand to Catalina. She grasped it lightly. In a wave of color and motion, her image changed from ghostly to human. Without hesitating, she stepped away from the land of the dead.

Marisol and Racquel smiled as well, knowing that Diego had made the right choice. Marisol hugged Racquel, giving her a little kiss on the forehead. Then she rushed forward and jumped into Catalina's body. She joined her mind and spirit to hers. The two women became one entity, although by all outward appearances, people would recognize Catalina if they saw her walking down the street.

Magnifico cocked his right eye at Sullivan. When the man returned the look, the dragon nodded once. Sullivan did the same, feeling a fierce pride for his latest choice.

"Don't be afraid, Diego," said Racquel. "I'm sure we'll see each other again in the future."

"How?"

"I'm not really sure. I just have this feeling that our time together isn't over."

"I hope not, Racquel."

"Goodbye, for now," she said. "Give my best to your family, and to those two rascals, Ricardo and Jose."

"Wait!' said Diego. "What about your family? What can we tell them, that their daughter disappeared overnight with a giant, talking dragon?"

Racquel glanced at Magnifico. Then she turned and walked away from everything she knew in her world. In seconds, her body faded away. All that remained was the silent soil of the riding ring.

"Don't worry, Diego," said Magnifico. "Everything will be explained in the morning. It is time we all returned to our homes."

Sullivan climbed aboard Magnifico. He slapped the same spike Diego held to balance himself during flight. Instantly, Magnifico stood. He began flapping his wings gently, stretching them for his next journey. Sullivan looked down at the small boy peering up at him.

"Be proud of yourself," he said. "You were asked to assume responsibility for a great journey, Diego. Your parents would be pleased."

Diego smiled and then the grin turned to painful realization. "My parents!"

CHAPTER THIRTY

Diego ran all the way home. He felt certain that when he rounded the corner by his driveway, his father would be outside waiting for him. As he ran by the homes on his block, he felt a surge of relief. Somehow, the night had lasted much longer than usual. He said a silent prayer for Racquel as he unlocked the gate by their pool.

Diego snuck into his room just before his mother arose from her bed. He kicked off his shoes, yanked his jacket and gloves off, and dove under the covers. A second after he closed his eyes his mother cracked open the door to his bedroom.

Diego's heart hammered in his chest. If his mother had come into his room to check on him, she would have known something was up instantly. Fortunately, she pulled the door shut as quietly as she could. Diego exhaled a mighty breath, and moments later, he fell fast asleep.

CHAPTER THIRTY-ONE

Esteban Ramirez rolled over and rubbed his eyes. The sun seemed especially bright for some reason. He kept his eyes shaded behind his hands until they grew accustomed to the light. He sat up, yawned, and scraped the dirt and sticks from his hair. Blinking a few times, he did his best to remember where he had finally lain down to sleep the night before.

The noises of the dawn workers shook his memory. He peeked over the barrier atop the supermarket. The whiny, corrugated metal door had been raised. Trucks delivering loads of produce, groceries, meats, fowl, and fish lined up behind each other. Esteban leaned back over, lying down on the inside of the top tier of the roof.

He had found the location by accident one night. While stumbling through the wee hours of the morning, he had leaned against the outer wall of the market. His hand wrapped around something cool, and that was when he saw the steel utility ladder running up the wall. Even with the lower half covered by a locked, steel panel, Esteban found that if he stretched as high as he could, he could just reach the first unprotected rung. Afterward, when he could scale the building without being noticed, he climbed the ladder to his hiding place and slept soundly. Very few people disturbed him in his makeshift crow's nest.

He pushed his hand into his pants pocket, pulling out the few coins he managed to save from the previous night's drinking. *One dollar and nine cents,* he thought to himself, *barely enough for a small doughnut and coffee.* He straightened his socks before slipping on his shoes. He stood, still somewhat wobbly from the effects of the alcohol.

He looked over the railing again, checking on the progress of the delivery trucks. His head swayed, the sure sign of a messy hangover on its way through his system. *Another fifteen minutes,* he thought, *after that they should be gone.*

CHAPTER THIRTY-TWO

Mickey's donuts opened promptly at five in the morning. The proprietors arrived at two-thirty, when most of the city lay dead asleep.

Catalina Alvarez rapped on the glass door at four forty-five. When the woman rolling out dough looked up, Catalina waved and smiled. The flour-coated woman smiled back, walked around the counter and let her in.

As she had for the past week since being hired, Catalina moved smoothly around the room, wiping down the tables and chairs with a damp washcloth. She refilled sugar containers and made sure the stacks of free newspapers stood straight and proper in their racks. After that, she started three coffee pots, one for regular, one for decaf, and the last for hot tea. She set creamers on the counter and made certain there were enough tissues and bags close by. After everything looked right, she went to the back and retrieved the cash drawer. She counted it in front of the owner before bringing it to the register. At four fifty-nine, she took the keys and opened the door. She flipped the open/closed sign over and went back to her side of the counter.

Sure as the sunrise, the first group through the door were the conversadors, as she called them. Five men, all in their seventies at least, arrived every morning like clockwork. They bought exactly the same donuts, had their coffee poured to their liking, and then sat at the same table discussing the affairs of the day.

"Good morning, Mr. Harrod," said Catalina, smiling.

"If I had no other reason to get out of bed," he said in response, "I'd do so just to see your pretty smile."

Catalina beamed as she prepared his order. She greeted the other men as well, talking smoothly with each as she rang up their purchases.

"Did the owner give you a raise, yet, like I suggested?" asked Mr. Atherton. The shop owner smiled at the statement as she inserted a tray of fresh donuts into the glass case.

"You know I've been here only one week," said Catalina sweetly.

You could hear the next group of customers ten feet before they got to the door. They were a group of rabble-rousers who worked through the night and into the wee hours stocking groceries and yelling obscenities at each other. The crew chief, always in the lead, yanked the donut shop door open so hard the hinges groaned. The elderly men stopped their conversations briefly, looking over at the group of disheveled, filthy workers. The crew chief hailed the men, wishing them a good morning.

"Good day, youngsters," answered the men.

"Everything safe with the world?" one of the crew asked.

"As long as the store is still standing," a man said, laughing.

The crew chief smiled a devilish smile, stepping in front of the others to place his order.

As she reached under the glass to retrieve his donuts, Catalina glanced at the front door. She saw a handsome young man staggering on the sidewalk toward the store. Just as he reached out to grasp the handle, he bent over and gripped his stomach.

Grimacing with pain, hunger, or sickness, Catalina didn't know, the stranger released the handle and fell to his knees on the sidewalk.

"Please, help him," she pleaded.

The night crew rushed outside. They grabbed Esteban, laughing at the stench of whiskey pouring from his gaping mouth.

"He'd be perfect for the night crew," said one of the young men, causing the rest to laugh again. They carried him inside and deposited him into a chair at a table in the far corner of the shop.

The crew shuffled outside to the patio, talking and laughing about another in a long line of drunks or drug abusers they had seen during their years at the store.

Catalina tossed their cash into the drawer, closed it, and hustled over to the young man. "Hello," she said as she squatted low in front of Esteban. "Are you all right?"

Esteban shoved his hand into his pants pocket and produced his small pile of change. "Coffee," he said, his eyes closed.

"I asked if you are okay," she asked again.

Esteban looked at her for the first time. No one had asked about his well-being for so long. He almost broke down in tears right then and there. "I-I'm okay," he said, holding his hand in front of his mouth.

"Is this all the money you have?" asked Catalina.

Esteban seemed embarrassed to answer the question. He nodded sheepishly.

"Stay here," she said. "You need something to eat. Catalina went behind the counter and grabbed two donuts, a maple bar and a chocolate bar. She placed them in a basket and then poured a large coffee. She rung up the sale, threw his coins into the slots, and added some money of her own.

"This isn't a proper breakfast, but we'll take care of that later. Just sit, eat, and enjoy the coffee. I have some work to do."

Marisol peered through Catalina's eyes. She looked at Esteban, knowing in her heart he would be loved deeply by the young woman whose soul she shared.

"Do you promise to stay here until we can talk again?"

"Why are you being nice to me?" he asked. "What's your name?"

"My name is Catalina," she said, "and you are destined for greater things than sleeping in the streets."

This time the tears did come. He tried hard to hold tight, but it had been so long since anyone had shown him kindness.

"It's okay," she cooed. "Everything's going to be okay from now on. Please, tell me your name."

"Esteban. My name's Esteban."

CHAPTER THIRTY-THREE

Diego tumbled into a pleasant dream. There were no fires, no dreadful dragons, and no heroes from the past. He saw a large family gathering, much like the one his parents hosted after he'd won the writing contest. Even though at first glance he recognized no one, he felt welcome in the home. One by one, people reached their hands out to him, smiling and thanking him for his courage. He recognized many generations of a single family. This fiesta certainly held great meaning for them.

"Diego!" shouted a familiar voice. "Diego. Over here!"

He turned his head and saw Racquel. He ran to her, and she to him. She threw her arms around him, thanking him as the others had done. She released him and looked into his eyes. Her smile beamed brighter than ever.

"This is my family, Diego. You brought them home."

"All of these people, they were all in the desert?"

"Yes," said Racquel. "Many mothers, fathers, and children died trying to cross the border. Some of them wandered the desert for decades waiting for someone to bring them home. You did that, Diego, and they'll praise you for it always."

Diego felt loving warmth spreading throughout his body. As quickly as it began, though, selfish thoughts about Racquel smothered it like a wet blanket thrown over dying embers.

"Can you come home, now? He asked. "Have you completed your part in our journey?"

"I can't, Diego. Don't you see? It was my sacrifice and your bravery that allowed Magnifico and the other dragons to help us find our way. Without everyone playing their part, my family and the rest of the spirits would forever be roaming the desert.

"I made a deal with Mr. Sullivan and Magnifico very early on. I would give my life for my family, and they would see to it that the proper guide would help them come home."

Diego understood, but his mood sagged anyway. He would miss seeing Racquel's smiling face at school every day. He looked at her eyes, and the question that lay within them.

"Aren't you interested in who Catalina is, and what she's doing right now?" she asked.

He'd forgotten about her, the stranger he'd chosen to come back to the world of the living.

"She's a distant cousin of mine," said Racquel. "She followed her lover into the desert. They wanted a new life together, and she believed in him."

"That's terrible," said Diego. "All those people."

"But they're safe now, Diego, because of you, and Catalina is helping Esteban find himself again. You'll see, in time you'll understand just how important you've been to your people."

"Like the heroes of our past?"

"Si, Corazón. They helped us in their time, and you've done so in ours."

"Will I see you again?" he asked.

"I'm sure we'll see each other soon, Diego. Now return to your sleep. You need rest. You've had a busy time these last few weeks."

He heard Racquel's family cheering their young hero. Diego waved back. He hugged Racquel, kissed her cheek, and said his goodbyes. In the distant sky, he heard the roar of a mighty dragon. He looked up, smiling.

"Hasta Luego, Magnifico."